Of Magic and The Sea

Addison Kayne

Of Magic and The Sea

Cover Design
www.yocladesigns.com

Dear Reader:

My editor, proofreader, and I carefully proofread each of my books before publication. We work hard to produce ebooks that are 100% free of typographical errors. But typos are sneaky little devils, and sometimes they slip past us. If you spot any of those devils lurking in the book, please visit http://www.AddisonKayne.com to email them to me. Thank you! Together, we can stamp out sneaky typos!

DEDICATION

To Kevin, my one true love. Thank you for giving me the freedom to build castles in the air; and the courage to soar high above them on the wings of a dragon. I will love you forever and beyond.

CHAPTER ONE

University of Connecticut, Present Day

Brenna Sinclair dismissed her students and watched them skitter out of the lecture hall like mice, each one vying for the lead.

Her efforts to collect her notes and books and stuff them into her briefcase faltered when a wave of dizziness swept over her. She grabbed the podium with both hands and steadied herself. Tiny droplets of sweat beaded at her temple, and her stomach roiled like an angry sea. She closed her eyes and fought to control her rapid, shallow breathing.

Oh no, not now. Please not now.

"Professor Sinclair! Are you all right?" Daniel was the mouse who'd lost his way at the end of class. He ran up the stairs to the lectern and grabbed an elbow to stay her swaying.

"I'm okay. I just need to sit for a minute."

Daniel eased her into a chair and continued to question her, but his voice faded and the dizziness worsened. This vision was going to be a doozie. With no other choice, she closed her eyes, and let the images play like a movie on the back of her eyelids.

Torchlight flickered, casting dancing shadows throughout the cavern. Water rushed in, spewing raging threats to the man trapped in its fury. His wrists were manacled to the stone wall at his back, arms stretched out from his body. The muscles of his bare chest rippled with the exertion of pulling against his bindings. Her first glimpse of the man tilted her world off its axis and set off a tsunami of emotions. Anguish. Heartbreak. Desire.

The watermark on the wall of the cavern left no doubt he'd drown. And she would watch him die.

"I am with you," Brenna whispered.

The man's head snapped back, and his eyes scanned the shadowy cavern.

"Where are ye lass? I can't see ye," he rasped, his voice richly toned with a Scottish burr.

"I'm not in the cavern with you. I see you. . .with my mind. While our minds are connected, we share a bond," Brenna said. She swallowed the lump in her throat.

When the man looked precisely in her direction as she spoke, it unnerved her. The link she shared was always one way. She could see those who reached out for her and their surroundings as if she were right there with them, but they could never see her. She slid her hand up her cheek and covered the ragged scar that stretched from her eye to the corner of her mouth in a furious arc.

"I don't think yer mind will be much help in my predicament. Truly, it's better if yer not here."

He was right. The water advanced to slay its prey, and the undertow ripped away precious time.

"I'll stay with you. You'll not die alone," Brenna said.

Corded muscles rippled along the length of powerful arms. He fisted his hands and a warmth pooled low in her belly. He had extraordinary green eyes, lush and soft as a springtime meadow. They held her still and silent. Her breath hitched and something shifted within the confines of her soul. The water reached his jaw. He arched his head back as far as he could and fought to keep the water at bay.

"I've been alone for a very long time. I thank ye for staying."

"Is there a message I can give to your family?" Brenna asked.

"Aye, tell Clan MacGregor that Lachlan Alexander Stuart MacGregor has not given up hope that they will find me and free me from this wretched hell!"

Brenna stifled the urge to tell him his request made no sense. His only freedom would come when his body succumbed to an angry sea and his soul departed for an unknown fate.

Lachlan struggled against the shackles. Failing to break the bonds, he loosed an anguished bellow so wretched that Brenna slid off her chair and hit the floor on her knees. Clasping her hands over her ears, she tried to silence the sound of Lachlan's suffering.

"Professor Sinclair, please, can you hear me?" Daniel asked.

The vision faded away like smoke in a breeze.

Brenna shook her head to clear the image of Lachlan's suffering from her mind. Her heart beat a bass drum in her chest, and she fought to catch her breath. A single tear slid from her eye and she banished it with the back of her hand. "I'm okay. This has been happening to me most of my life. I'm fine now, really."

Brenna attempted to convince herself it was true as the dizziness lessened and she became aware of her surroundings once again.

But she wasn't all right. She'd just watched a man lose his battle against the sea. Lachlan MacGregor was not the first man she'd watched die. And he likely wasn't going to be the last. This time, it was different. The connection they'd shared, however brief, had been profound and heart wrenching. She still felt it, a part of him, like an electric current sending sizzling sparks zinging through her body.

"Your color is coming back. Are you feeling better?" The wide eyes and shocked look on Daniel's face revealed his fear for her. "Here, let me help you up. I'll walk you back to your office." He took hold of her arms and pulled her to her feet.

"Thanks. I appreciate your help."

"What did you mean when you said this has been happening most of your life? Are you ill?" Daniel finished stuffing her lecture notes into her briefcase.

"Oh, no. . .not ill exactly. Low blood sugar." Most people believed her standard excuse. "Makes me dizzy, and I have spells where I faint, or come close to it. I'm glad you kept me from falling on my face," she said and avoided his eyes.

“Hypoglycemic, huh? You sounded like you were in terrible pain.”

He led the way down the hallway and outside into the fresh air. Obviously, he didn’t buy her story. She quickened her step and searched for a response that would put an end to the question and answer session. Not just any explanation would satisfy the smartest student in her class.

“My ears ring something fierce when one of these dizzy spells comes on,” she lied. She wanted nothing more than to escape to the solace of her office and down a handful of ibuprofen to cease the pounding in her head. Daniel quirked an eyebrow and mulled over her answer. They walked in silence until the squat three-story building that housed her office emerged at the end of the tree-lined walkway like a beacon.

“I’ll be fine from here. Thanks for the escort. I’ll see you next week for the final exam.” Brenna reached for her briefcase and books, and though Daniel gave her a quizzical look, he relinquished her belongings.

She trekked up the stairs to the sanctity of her office in the psych building and collapsed into her chair. *Just breathe. You can do this, keep calm and carry on. Lachlan MacGregor, wherever you are now, I’m sorry I couldn’t save you. I hope the heavens have welcomed you home.*

A whirlwind of activity at her feet interrupted her thoughts. Merlin, her Chihuahua and the department mascot, danced around her ankles for attention. Too cute for his own good, the blue and cream imp had won the heart of the department director. Certain university policies had been bent, and the little tyke was granted the right to share an office with his mistress. He made the gargantuan leap into her lap and flopped onto his back for a belly rub, and she indulged him.

The world outside her window appeared serene and ordinary, a stark contrast to the fragmented thoughts crashing together in her mind like a tempest. Why? Why did she feel like the Grim Reaper had ripped her heart from her chest?

The air inside her office was stagnant, and a feeling of suffocation had Brenna plopping Merlin from her lap to the chair as she hauled herself up to open the window. She inhaled the calming scent of the lilac bush just outside, its pale lavender flowers coaxed into blooming by the warm spring breeze. Tomorrow, she would clip a few sprigs to put in a vase on her desk but right now, she had a promise to keep. Relaying a message to a dead man's family.

The laptop on her desk had slipped into sleep mode. A touch of her finger, and the machine flickered to life. She settled next to Merlin in the leather chair at her desk. Uncertain where to begin her search for Lachlan's family, Brenna hoped the almighty Google god would be good to her.

A rainbow of blank notebooks was stacked neatly on the corner of her desk. The one with the black cover fit her mood and she pulled it from the middle of the stack. She slid the black pen from its spine, flipped it open, and readied it for notes. She lost herself in research until the glare on the computer screen indicated the sun had begun its late afternoon trek through the western part of the sky. Clan MacGregor had their roots in the Highlands of Scotland along the eastern border of Argyle and the western border of Perthshire. Judging by their history, the MacGregors had lived an unruly, marauding life.

She pushed away from her desk and stood, stretching her arms above her head. A groan escaped as she worked out the kinks from sitting. The research had turned up only one man by the name of Lachlan Alexander Stuart MacGregor, and if the source was correct, that man had died in the year 1394. There was nothing mentioned of his namesake, the man she'd watched drown just hours before.

Tension from the morning's vision lingered, and the headache continued to pound. An uneasy knot quivered in her stomach. Learning the history of the MacGregor clan was easy. Finding Lachlan's branch of the family was proving to be difficult.

The laptop screen faded into hibernation mode. Head back and eyes closed, Brenna drifted toward oblivion until the rhythmic tap of high heels in the hallway startled her.

Shit. Fashion police.

Brenna ripped out the number two pencil holding her makeshift bun in place. She let her long auburn tresses fall in their usual riotous waves down her back. She swept her hair in front of her shoulders, and ran her hands over her favorite white shirt, hoping to smooth the wrinkles that creased the garment. She was not in the mood for a lecture on her inability to dress like an esteemed member of the faculty. Shrugging out of her navy blue jacket, she tossed it across the room. It landed in a heap on her couch.

Jen walked in, a takeout bag from the Blue Moon Deli in her hand. "Nice try, Brenna, but I know that jacket has enough dog hair on it to knit a sweater. Daniel was concerned about you. He told me about what happened this morning. Out with the details." Jen opened the deli bag and handed her a sandwich.

Jennifer Baker was not only an administrative assistant for the professors in the psych department, but also her only friend. People with psychic visions had surprisingly few friends. At least that had been Brenna's experience. Over the years she'd learned to hide the disturbing visions as much as possible, but Jen didn't flinch at the freakish episodes.

Unwrapping the pastrami on rye, Brenna took a bite while contemplating what to say. Jen waited patiently for her to begin. They had been through this routine a hundred times before, but it never seemed to get any easier for Brenna to purge herself of a vision.

Each one was the same, yet different. Those who reached out to her were the most desperate people in the direst of circumstances. Brenna's mind picked out their pleas for help as if from the collective consciousness of the world. She'd helped them. All of them. Until a brush with death changed her thinking.

"Come on, out with it," Jen said.

"I couldn't save him." It was that simple.

After taking another bite of her sandwich and then popping the top of a Dr. Pepper, Brenna filled Jen in on the details.

"Held in a cavern, huh?" Jen picked imaginary lint from her pristine black trousers. "So, he was murdered?"

"I suppose he was." Brenna sipped her soda. "He told me to tell Clan MacGregor that Lachlan Alexander Stuart MacGregor had not given up hope that his family would find him and free him from his wretched hell. How can a man be moments from death and believe that his family will find him and free him? It makes no sense."

"I don't know. That is an odd thing to say."

Brenna checked her watch. “Listen, I need to get out of here and get some fresh air.” She rewrapped the remains of her pastrami sandwich, tucked the laptop under her arm, and hustled toward the door. “Merlin, get your leash. Let’s go.”

The critter scampered to the wicker basket on the floor by the door. He sat down and looked at Brenna, then back at his basket of toys. Clearly, he debated whether to follow instructions or grab a toy instead. In the end, he managed both. He preceded Brenna out the door and trotted down the hall with his leash dangling from one side of his mouth, a toy from the other.

CHAPTER TWO

Brenna walked into the cool stable, drawing a deep breath. The pungent aroma of hay and horses filled the air, melting away the stress that lingered from the previous day's vision. The night had been dreadful. She had only drifted on the fringes of sleep, kept there by hauntingly green eyes and a Scottish brogue she'd never forget. The last minutes of Lachlan's life replayed in her mind like a scratched record. Over and over again, she found herself mesmerized by the longing in his eyes and the baritone timbre of his voice.

Brenna heard the tires from Jen's little Fiat spit gravel as she presumably slid the car into a parking space. Jen was only half an hour late.

Pushing aside her thoughts of Lachlan, Brenna grabbed the reins and led Fitzroy and Ginger out into the crisp morning air. Fitzroy, a handsome chestnut gelding, stood sixteen hands, and had earned a solid reputation for schmoozing female riders. Given the chance, he would lead a novice rider astray. Brenna loved his spirited nature. He was a challenge and a joy to ride for anyone who'd experienced considerable time in the saddle.

Ginger. Well, little Ginger at thirteen hands was perfect for Jen, who was content to mosey along the trail, designer coffee in hand, and not have to worry about anything unexpected happening.

Jen slapped a hand on her hip and gave her a once over look. "You look like hell, Brenna."

"Thanks. I can always count on you to boost my ego." Brenna sighed, but she offered her friend a forgiving smile. "And you're late. Again."

"I know, I'm sorry, but you wouldn't believe the line at Starbucks. Besides, I'm always late, you know that."

As usual, Jen looked impeccably turned out. Her long golden hair was fixed in a tight French braid that must have taken a lifetime of practice to perfect. Her jodhpurs and riding jacket didn't have a smudge or speck of dust anywhere, and her English riding boots would shame a spotless mirror. Ruby red lipstick and Ray-Ban sunglasses completed her ensemble.

"Long or short trail today?" Jen asked.

"Short trail. I want to get back to researching Lachlan's family. For a dead man, he kept me awake all night. I can't shake the feeling that a part of him is still with me."

Jen's brows rose over her Ray-Bans. "It's not like you knew the guy. There wasn't anything you could have done, so don't get hung up on the guilt."

"I'll rest easier once I can tell his family what happened, if they'll even believe me."

Brenna dutifully held Jen's supersized white chocolate mocha so she could mount her sturdy little mare. Once Jen was settled, Brenna walked to the boot scraper and removed the offending horse shit from her fifteen-year-old Durango boots. She wanted no complaints from Jen and couldn't stomach the thought of her friend wrinkling her pert little nose for the duration of their ride.

The trail began with a wide dirt path that allowed Fitzroy and Ginger plenty of room to walk side by side. The oak trees flanking the trail would form a thick canopy of leaves once they finished bursting forth to greet the later days of spring. Robins rummaged the ground for morning worms, and blue jays squawked in the trees overhead. Grey squirrels flittered across the trail ahead, tails switching apprehensively at the approach of riders on horseback.

"I'm heading for the meadow to give Fitzroy a bit of a workout. Catch up when you can," Brenna said with a slight touch to the gelding's flanks. Raising her white chocolate mocha in a silent toast, Jen continued to poke along.

Unlike race car drivers who earned their living making a series of left hand turns, Fitzroy pounded the ground at a flat out gallop along the edge of the field, making right hand turns in rapid succession. Joyful abandon flowed through Brenna like a tidal wave. Her spirits soared with each lap around the meadow. Lying low across his back, she urged him to run faster. Horse and rider had made half a dozen circuits around the field when Jen finally appeared.

A wave of dizziness struck and Brenna's joy faded in a flash. The ragged scar that marred the left side of her face thrummed in tune with the beat of her heart. The rest of her face tingled and tiny rivulets of sweat wound their way from her temple to her jaw. Another vision forced its way in front of her eyes.

Brenna pulled back hard on the reins. Fitzroy reared up, and Brenna couldn't hold on. She slipped from the saddle and hit the ground, her shoulder taking the impact. Fitzroy came perilously close to stomping on her as he pranced wildly in circles around her huddled form. A cry escaped her, and she lifted her head to search for Jen.

The half full designer coffee flew over Jen's shoulder as her heels kicked Ginger's flanks harshly in her haste to reach Brenna.

Fitzroy bolted when Jennifer dismounted. She ran the last few feet to Brenna.

"What is it? Are you hurt? Is it a vision?"

Brenna's eyes closed tightly, and she nodded, rolled onto her back, and reached for Jen's hand.

Torches burned and cast shadows on Lachlan's body. The raging waters of the day before had receded and left harmless puddles on the floor of the cavern.

His chin rested on his chest, long raven hair obscured the outline of his pale face. A faded and tattered plaid hung precariously at his waist.

Brenna's heart broke free of her chest and gagged her when it lodged in her throat.

"Is it ye then, lass? Have ye not had enough of watching me die that ye've come back for more?" Lachlan asked. He raised his head and tossed his hair out of his face. His mouth twitched upward and formed a tentative smile.

Brenna's throat cleared abruptly when her heart dislodged and rattled against her ribcage. Moments passed, and the mastodon sitting on her chest finally wandered away and allowed her to breathe.

She succumbed to the magnetism of his smile and reached out her hand to touch his cheek before she caught herself and pulled it back. One couldn't exactly reach across space and time to touch a vision, but an indescribable, undeniable knowing enfolded her in a warm embrace.

"How can this be? I felt the blankness of your mind as the water took you. You're…dead," Brenna said.

"Nay lass, not dead. I did drown, but this blasted immortality that plagues me refuses to let me die."

Immortal? Impossible.

Brenna's mind churned, but she couldn't fathom another explanation for why Lachlan lived. There had to be another reason. "Immortal? That explains why you think your family still had a chance at finding you."

"Aye, lass. I may be immortal, but I can't free myself from this place. There is magic cast here. It runs through these manacles and strips me of my powers. An old and powerful magic wielded by my enemy to keep me here for eternity."

The hair on her arms stood in battle formation. Breathing became more difficult as her blood pressure ticked up several notches.

"So, exactly what type of immortal being are you? Vampire, werewolf, a warlock perhaps?" A hint of sarcasm marked her words.

Immortal? Still not buying it. Magic? Madness.

"I was born of a mortal woman, and my sire is king of the Faerie Realm."

"King of the Fairy? As in little folk? You're a fairy?"

"Half Fae."

Brenna hugged her middle, fighting back the giggles that silently wracked her body. Thankfully, with their minds linked, Lachlan could only hear, not see her inappropriate stress reaction.

Lachlan raised an eyebrow and waited for Brenna to respond to his declaration.

"Lass?"

"Yes, well, that's certainly better than the other alternatives. I would have thought you'd be smaller, being a fairy." He could have come up with a more plausible lie.

Both eyebrows went up and hit the stratosphere at that comment, and Brenna couldn't tell if his eyes held annoyance or amusement.

"Bloody hell, lass. I'm not a pixie or a sprite. I'm a Fae prince. Although, a bastard."

Brenna's inappropriate laugh, though silent, shamed her into lowering her head and covering her scar with her palm.

"It's all right, lass. A common enough mistake. No need for ye to fret over it."

A fairy and a gentleman.

"You said you can't free yourself. Is there something I can do to help you?" The words tumbled from her mouth before she thought twice about her offer to help.

Dammit.

That was absolutely the last thing she'd intended to do. She wouldn't play in another game of life or death. She wouldn't be used or maimed or worse.

"There have to be MacGregor's who know of me. Ye must simply find one. Then between ye, find my father, King Ratava, or my sister, Princess Ariel. They are the only two people I trust."

"Lachlan, I'm the only one who even knows you exist. Like it or not, you'll have to trust me as well." Her voice held a sharp edge as her frustration with herself bubbled to the surface. "And besides, I can't—"

"Begin the search at Castle MacGregor in the Highlands of Scotland," Lachlan said.

Brenna shut her eyes and inhaled deeply, centering herself. Yes, she would once again be just a pawn, this time taking orders from a half-bastard fairy.

Brenna's eyes snapped open, and she found Jen kneeling next to her holding her hand tightly. Concern flared from Jen's sapphire eyes.

"He's alive, Jen."

"Who's alive? You can't mean the dead guy from yesterday?"

Brenna nodded.

"What did he do, hold his breath until the tide went out?" Jen asked.

"No. Says he's immortal. A bastard fairy to be exact."

"A what? You're telling me he's not human? Are you back on those prescription sleeping pills? 'Cause you're dreaming, girlfriend."

"I know how this sounds, but I'm telling you, he's alive."

"Right. A fairy. Is he a good fairy or a bad fairy? No, let me guess, must be a bad one. Why else would someone chain him up and leave him for dead?"

Brenna rolled her eyes at Jen's sarcasm and sat up. She swatted at the grass stain on her worn jeans. Another pair ruined.

"I offered to help him, Jen."

Jen flinched as if she'd been slapped. "The last time almost killed you. You ended up with that horrible scar on your cheek and the guy ended up dead. What if he's a bad fairy?"

"I know, I know. The words just flew out of my mouth. I wasn't thinking. He's alive, Jen. I can't believe it, but he's alive. And he's not bad."

"What? How can you know that? You know nothing about him."

"Trust me. I just know." Profound peace settled over her like angel wings.

Jen huffed with annoyance and went in search of her horse.

CHAPTER THREE

Highlands of Scotland, Present Day

The torches on either side of Lachlan cast curious shadows on the cavern wall. Faerie magic kept the flames alive. The years of captivity made it effortless for his mind to slip from his harsh reality into the world of his imagination. His flights into fantasy kept him from falling into madness, though barely. His mind conjured images from the flickering torchlight and gave them the appearance of reality.

A trick of the torchlight cast a shadow on the cavern wall and Lachlan's favorite illusion took shape. A woman he'd dubbed his shadow dancer brought him comfort in his darkest hours. The shadow danced and stayed with him as the tide began its inevitable rise. She wrapped her fingers behind her neck and twisted her long hair around her hand, lifting it off her shoulders. She closed her eyes and her hips began a sultry sway, moving to the music that only he could hear. She never failed to ease the torment of the tide when it came for him.

The water's slow march sounded long before it reached him. The rise and fall of the echo matched the cadence of the waves and grew steadily louder.

Lachlan sucked in his breath at the first touch of the icy Atlantic on his bare feet. The tiny tentacles of pain turned slowly to a more welcome numbness as it crept upward past his chained ankles.

His mind wandered to other pleasant thoughts. So many years had passed in the cavern, he was no longer sure if the thoughts were memories or solace his imagination conceived to help him endure the endless days and nights of his prison.

He inhaled deeply of the salt tinged air, but smelled instead the pungent burning of a peat fire in the great hall of his castle. He felt a wolfhound at his feet and tasted fine Scotch whiskey burning low in his belly, spreading its warmth, and melting the ice from his bones.

The water crept higher, and he searched for a memory of Beltane. Great bonfires burned to mark the time of purification and transition, the celebration signifying a hope that the new season would bring fruitful harvests later in the year. Feasting, drinking, and merry-making heralded the first light of morning as livestock were ushered into summer pastures for grazing.

Gooseflesh erupted across his chest as the water reached his waist. After all this time, he still had to fight off the claustrophobic grip of the cloying, drunken wench that was the water. He steadied his breath, his mind slipped away from his present existence, and he felt for a moment the weight of Senga, his gyrfalcon perching on his leather wrapped wrist. He fisted his hand around the jesses to steady her and realized with a start, she was gone.

His memories no longer distracted him from his inevitable death. There would be no escape this day. He inhaled deeply, this time the salt-tinged water. It constricted his throat and filled his lungs. He choked out his final breath and let the water take him. Again.

###

Brenna woke in a fit of coughing and sat up abruptly, her throat raw and her tongue tasting of salt. Waves of tingles ran down her arms and legs and forced her to remain motionless until the remnants of a dizzy spell passed. Merlin peeked from the covers. He looked thoroughly disheveled and made known his displeasure with a growl.

"Shhh, Merlin. Go back to sleep." He huffed and crawled back under the comforter.

Brenna tried to recall the last bits of the dream that had stolen the breath from her lungs.

Lachlan.

But, it hadn't been a dream. It had been a surreal vision of a drowning man.

She fisted her hands and rubbed the unexpected tears from her eyes. The bitter taste of the sea burned the back of her throat. She lay back down and waited impatiently for the waterworks to cease and the fog to clear from her thoughts. Was this her fate? To watch Lachlan drown with each high tide? Her heart constricted and she cringed. Well, so much for sleeping in this morning.

"Come on, Merlin, time for breakfast."

The announcement brought the little imp out from under the covers, this time with enthusiasm. He stretched, yawned, and licked Brenna's cheek, and then he was off to wait in the kitchen by his bowl.

She padded barefoot down the stairs. The smell of raspberry-chocolate coffee wafted from her automatic pot and pulled her like a magnet. The scrambled eggs she whipped up turned out a bit dry, but the English muffin came out precisely the way she preferred. Perfectly charred around the edges.

"What are we going to do about Lachlan?" she asked Merlin.

She looked over her shoulder and saw Merlin had grown tired of waiting for his breakfast. Napping in the slice of sunlight streaming in through the sliding door, he opened one beady little brown eye enough to assure Brenna he was listening.

"I've never had visions like this before. How can I wake up, taste salt water and barely breathe at exactly the same moment when Lachlan drowns?"

Pondering the strangeness of the connection she shared with Lachlan, she took out two plates from the cupboard and portioned the eggs between them, sprinkling Parmesan cheese over both. She quartered the burnt muffin and added Merlin's portion to his plate. Why she ever bothered to buy him a bowl she couldn't recall. He ate most of his meals off her Fiestaware, and that suited them both just fine. The fiend swaggered over the moment his plate hit the floor and licked it clean before she could grab herself a fork and sit down.

The whack of the doggie door a moment later indicated Merlin had gone outside to enjoy the morning sun and wait for unsuspecting insects to invade his territory.

Brenna puttered around her townhome for another hour, waiting for the tide to recede enough so she could reach for Lachlan. An hour didn't seem like enough time for him to recover so she headed upstairs to shower.

The hot water did little to slow the racing thoughts occupying her mind, but did ease some of the tension from her neck and shoulders. She stood for a long time, forehead against the shower wall. Just how far would she go to help a stranger?

The Highlands of Scotland. Beautiful and sacred, wild and enchanting. Castles crowning splintered crags, narrow glens carpeted in heather, and water horses emerging from the steely depths of the lochs issuing their fatal challenge to mount and ride. Anything was possible in the Highlands. Lachlan was proof of it.

Scantily clad men in skirts. A check for the go column.

A chance to run her hands over Lachlan's body and feel his muscles contract beneath her touch, easing the aches and pains caused from his inability to move freely. Definitely another check for the go column.

Death, dismemberment, and failure. Three checks for the no column.

She finally reached down and turned the cold water on full blast. The icy temperature chilled her, but the gooseflesh rippling up her arms and down her legs came from something else altogether. She shut off the flow of water, stepped briskly out of the shower, and toweled off her hair. She wrapped the towel around her and tucked in the end at her breast, attempting to determine the source of her unease.

“Lass, I’ve tried to keep from troubling ye, but there are two things I would know,” Lachlan said.

Lachlan. She jumped at the sound of his voice in her head. His words barely registered. This was the first time in all her years of visions that one hadn’t been preceded by a wave of dizziness.

“Lass? Are ye there?”

“Yes, I mean, two things?”

“Yer name, lass. I would have yer name.”

Brenna smiled at the oversight. She knew his full name, had researched the history of Clan MacGregor, and learned Lachlan was a bastard half-mortal Fae prince. He knew nothing of her except the sound of her voice in his head. “Brenna. My name is Brenna Sinclair.”

Brenna crossed the oak floor of her bathroom, leaving droplets of water from her hair dripping in her wake. She threw off the towel when she reached her room and pulled out a pair of jeans and a t-shirt from the pile of clothes on her bedroom chair. The hooded look of Lachlan’s eyes startled her. No longer the color of a spring meadow, they transformed to a dark viridian. He dropped his eyes to the cavern floor.

Her eyes flickered across the broad expanse of his chest. Inching downward, her gaze followed the dusting of hair trailing below the plaid that barely hung onto his narrow hips. Her nipples pebbled at the sight of him.

Holy shit, stop staring. She couldn’t. The man rivaled Michelangelo’s David, at least what she could see of him.

She licked her lips reflexively and pulled her wandering thoughts together. “And the second thing you would like to know?”

“Are ye going to help me gain my freedom?”

She rifled through the pile looking for panties and came up empty-handed. Bouncing on her toes, she squiggled into her jeans then pulled on the wrinkled white tee.

She sat down on the edge of the king sized bed and hugged her knees, turning her toes under and rocking slightly while she formulated a response. Would it really be such a big deal to help him find his family?

Sidestepping the question, she unfolded her legs and reached for a hair clip on the nightstand beside her bed. Twisting her still wet uncombed hair, she lifted the heavy mass to the top of her head, clipped it into place, and resumed her rocking.

"First, there are things I need to know, Lachlan," she said, tapping a fingertip on her bottom lip, remembering Jen's words. "Tell me who chained you there, and why?"

He glanced in her direction. "My father was about to announce his successor to the throne. Our royal houses allow choice based on suitability rather than birthright or legitimacy. Because we are immortal, the crown passes to an heir every five hundred years. My half-brother feared our father would name me king. I had no interest in the position, but my brother believed otherwise. Now I wait upon the charity of another to gain my freedom." His hands fisted and pulled in defiance of the manacles.

He seemed embarrassed to make such a statement. He raised his head and the muscles of his jaw clenched. He straightened to his full height and waited for Brenna's words.

"I promised myself I would never again interfere in the circumstances of those with whom I share a vision. I made a mistake yesterday when I offered to help."

Lachlan's shoulders drooped and he dropped his chin to his chest. "Lass, please. Just find someone from my clan who knows of me. One who might find a way to get word to my sister or father. Is that really too much to ask of ye? Please. Save me from the madness that waits for me."

Brenna let go of her knees and flopped down on her back, spreading her arms like wings across the length of her bed. Was she an angel of mercy sent to free a tortured soul or just a psychic with a guilty conscience?

Despite her irritation with herself the day before, her resolve to keep the promise she had sworn to uphold above all others, wavered. Big time. She tried to be logical, not emotional.

"You seem like a good fairy, Lachlan. But I can't go off searching the Highlands for your family. I just can't." She felt her face flush and knew her guilty conscience would exert its influence. "I'll see what I can do from here."

Lachlan's broad mouth turned up in a smile that dazzled her. Her heart swelled, causing an unfamiliar ache, a longing she didn't understand.

###

Brenna lugged her laptop outside and spent the afternoon lounging in the patch of grass she called a backyard. Merlin, ever loyal, spent the time in her lap snuggled under her t-shirt. The only real success she had all day was in finding a man who claimed to be the Clan MacGregor historian, Colin MacGregor. Current proprietor of a B&B just a few miles from the historical seat of the clan, referred to simply as Castle MacGregor.

At the sound of the front door opening, Merlin struggled to free himself from the confines of Brenna's shirt, scampering for the door. It wasn't until that moment that Brenna realized the day had gotten away from her and it was nearly time for dinner.

"Jen, I'm out here," Brenna called out, flipping her laptop closed.

It was several minutes before Jen emerged from the house, two glasses of wine in hand. "Pasta's on." She handed a glass to Brenna. "How's Lachlan?"

"Better now. I decided I *am* going to help him."

Jennifer caught her breath at Brenna's words at precisely the same moment she swallowed a healthy sip of Cabernet. She blasted blood red wine onto the tender shoots of new grass at her feet. "Are you serious? I'm surprised you're thinking about doing this. What about your promise? You were nearly killed the last time you went chasing after a vision."

"I agreed to do what I could from here, no big deal. I'm not actually doing anything other than trying to pass on word of Lachlan's existence to someone who can help him. I'm just the messenger, and I am not breaking my promise."

"So you'll be staying on this side of the Atlantic and not traipsing off to Scotland?"

"Exactly right."

Jen's brows drew together in a frown. "What have you found out so far?"

"Not what, but whom. Colin MacGregor claims to be a MacGregor clan historian. I figure that's a good place to start," Brenna said. "And the sooner I contact him the better. I've been having a bit of an issue that I haven't had before. I woke up this morning coughing up salt water at exactly the same moment Lachlan drowned." Brenna watched her friend closely for her reaction.

"How long has this been happening?" Jen's eyes grew round, and she set down her wine glass on the wrought iron table with a *clink*.

"Since the first vision. A tightness in my chest; my lungs feeling like they're going to explode. Then this morning, the thing with the salt water." Brenna waved her hand in an attempt to be casual.

Jen shook her head and huffed out a breath. "So you're saying your connection with Lachlan is mental *and* physical? You're scaring me, girlfriend."

"I know. It's scary for me, too."

Jen seemed to weigh her words. "If the link to Lachlan is mental *and* physical, then you'd better think about getting your ass on a plane to Scotland. It could be more dangerous for you if you stay here. Unless of course, he's a bad fairy. Then you could be in more serious trouble if you go."

Brenna shook her head in denial of her friend's words.

"He's not a bad guy. He explained everything to me this morning. He has an ass for a brother and a serious case of wrong place at the wrong time, but he's a good man. Faerie."

Merlin's high-pitched bark interrupted their conversation. Brenna followed Jen into the kitchen to find the pasta water boiled over the edge of the pot. Merlin sat expectantly hoping something tasty might find its way to the floor.

Jen turned down the flame under the pot. "Your visions haven't always been pleasant, but you have a gift, Brenna. Maybe it is time to stop thinking of it as a curse and get back in the game. If he's truly an honorable man, he deserves your help."

CHAPTER FOUR

Brenna's forehead hit her desk with a *thunk*, and Merlin squiggled in her lap. "Sorry, buddy. Didn't mean to squish you. I suppose you're ready for a walk?"

Brenna lifted her head and swiveled her chair around. The magic words had Merlin leaping from her lap and scampering to his basket to collect his leash. He sat expectantly by the door and whimpered.

"Right. Let's go" Brenna rose from the chair and followed Merlin down the hall. She clicked his leash onto his collar and headed to a nearby campus courtyard. The air was fresh and invigorating and laced with the scent of grass. Brenna found a spot near an ancient oak and sat down pretzel style. She plucked at blades of grass, tearing them into thin strips, then flicking them away. Merlin rubbed his face in the spring shoots and finally lay contentedly beside her.

How exactly does one find the family of a Faerie prince? After three days of trying everything she could think of, the answer became painfully clear. One doesn't. Apparently, they don't have Facebook pages, Tumblr accounts, or Twitter in Faerie. Several emails to Colin MacGregor went unanswered and unreturned. Either the full moon or Mars in retrograde was thwarting her attempts to find Lachlan's family and give them the news he still lived.

She'd hoped the spring air would clear her mind and a brilliant thought would find its way into her head and an epiphany would occur.

Wrong.

She would have to tell Lachlan she'd failed. *Dammit.*

A light breeze ruffled her bangs and she leaned her head back against the trunk of the tree and closed her eyes. *Please let it be low tide.* Her mind quieted and settled and she reached for the connection they shared. It took a moment to find him. "Lachlan."

His head lifted from his chest and a smile cut across his chiseled features. A flutter rippled in her belly, and she imagined running her fingers through his ebony hair. Tracing a winding path down his spine and along the rise of his backside. Her eyes slid closed and her breath caught in her lungs.

"I've missed the sound of yer voice, lass. I'm glad yer here." The rich, deep sound soothed her nerves.

She took in a deep, even, deliberate breath and the words tumbled from her mouth. "I've had no luck finding your family. I've tried everything, and nothing has worked. I'm out of ideas. I've failed you, Lachlan. I just thought I'd let you know, there's nothing else I can do for you. I'm sorry." She closed her eyes against the sight of his sorrow at her words.

"Come to the Highlands."

Brenna scrubbed her face with her hands. The guilt card. Damn if she wasn't a sucker for the guilt card. A stack of final exams needed grading, but once they were finished, she would be a free woman for the summer.

Keep calm and carry on. Keep calm and carry on.

"There was another with whom I shared a connection," Lachlan said.

Another? There had been another. She swallowed hard and the green-eyed monster nudged her in the ribs. "What happened to her?"

"An accident took her life." His shoulders dropped and he stared at the cavern wall. "It was a long time ago. It took decades for me to find ye, Brenna. Come to the Highlands." His voice cracked.

So go to Scotland over the summer and try to find Lachlan's family? Or stay home and paint the kitchen, refinish the console she'd picked up at a flea market, and read the latest top ten on the NYT bestsellers list. Jen's words replayed in her mind. *A gift.* Maybe she should start using her psychic ability again. What if she could help him? Free him. Meet him in the flesh. The thought sent a torrent of chills from her head to her toes.

Oh, what the hell. What harm could come from a little trip across the pond?

"All right, Lachlan. I'll come to Scotland." The moment the words left her mouth, her heart lifted and relief flooded her. A puzzle piece fit soundly together in her soul. This was the right thing to do.

Lachlan's head fell back, and he let out a *whoop* of joy. A slow smile formed across his face. "Thank ye, Brenna."

"You're welcome. But I honestly don't think it's going to make a difference."

"Nay, lass. It has already made a difference. To me."

###

The incessant noise finally penetrated Colin MacGregor's consciousness, and he cracked open his eyes to find the black of night enshrouding him. He focused on the numbers glowing atop the nightstand. It was 1:06 AM. As in 1:06 in the fucking morning. He waited, presuming the racket would cease.

It didn't.

"Bloody hell."

He threw off the black down comforter and headed for his office down the hall, naked as a newborn. The light of the waning moon poured in through the unadorned windows bathing the room in a surreal silver glow.

He dropped into the chair behind his desk and shoved the phone between his ear and shoulder with a practiced calm he didn't feel. He had learned to deal with the discourteous travelers who couldn't manage to calculate they were calling him in the middle of the damn night. He simply charged them an extra £30 as an inconvenience factor.

"MacGregor B&B, Colin MacGregor speaking, how may I help ye?"

"Mr. MacGregor, I was afraid you wouldn't answer. It's rather late on your end isn't it? Brenna asked.

Colin raked a hand through his hair and rolled his eyes. "No, it's not late at all. It's bloody early here on my end." He dropped his head back against the cool leather chair and scrubbed his face with his hand, regretting his callous outburst. *Shit.*

“Ouch. Guess I deserved that comment. I’ve sent you a number of emails that you haven’t answered, so I thought I'd call. I’d like to make a reservation for a two week stay and talk with you about Lachlan MacGregor,” Brenna said.

The remaining vestiges of sleep vanished, and Colin’s irritation with the late night phone call immediately dissipated. He sat forward at the edge of his seat, elbows on his knees, processing what she’d just said.

“I’m sorry. I’ve been—away.” The full moon had wreaked havoc on him. “When will ye be arriving?” Colin asked.

“A day, maybe two, depending on the flights. I hope the short notice won’t be a problem?” she said.

“No problem at all. I’ll just need a faxed copy of yer driver’s license.”

“My license, Mr. MacGregor?” Colin could feel her glower at the other end of the line.

“No one has wanted to talk of Lachlan MacGregor in all my years as clan historian. I’d like to know for sure who’ll be asking the questions. Ye’ve just given me a day or two to find out what yer about,” Colin said.

“Then you know of Lachlan?”

“Aye, it’s my job to know. The real question is what do ye know of him?” The moments of silence on the other end of the line were deafening. “I think ye have no choice but to trust me. Spill what ye know.”

“He still lives,” Brenna whispered.

Colin drew in a long breath; a moment of agony hammered his chest for the misery Lachlan still endured. “The sooner ye get here, the sooner we can begin. Ye’ll fax me that document now, won’t ye?”

"Fine. I'll send it momentarily," Brenna said and hung up.

The phone fell away from Colin's ear, the cord catching on the forearm held up by his knee. The handset dangled from its cord like a hanged man. He hung it up, tugged on the chain of the green shaded banker's lamp sitting at the edge of his desk, and glared anxiously at the fax.

The machine squawked, and Colin saw her face for the first time. He yanked the fax off the contraption and bounded down the hall. He turned on every light of the great room where the tapestry hung.

There was no doubt.

It was she.

###

The tide began its inescapable rise. Out of habit, Lachlan focused his thoughts on the imaginary lass who had seen him through his battle with the sea thus far. His shadow dancer.

It was useless. Try as he might, he could not conjure her, and his thoughts returned to Brenna. He imagined her hair cascading down her back in waves. His mind quieted and it was she his imagination watched dance in the torchlight shadows of the cave.

The air in the cavern crackled with power and the hairs on the back of Lachlan's neck stood at attention. A sudden chill washed over him, colder than the frigid waters of the Atlantic. His mind must be more fragile than he imagined for a man appeared in front of him.

"It's been a long time, Lachlan. A century at least since someone has heard your pleas for freedom," said the man.

Lachlan's gaze turned to ice, and his muscles rippled as he instinctively reached for the throat of his keeper.

The man stepped closer, but stood an ocean away from Lachlan's manacled reach.

His brother.

Hafnar glared at Lachlan through whisky colored eyes. They might have been warm and inviting eyes but for the hatred that glazed them. Long strawberry blond hair fell thick and arrow-like past his shoulders. His nose was straight and regal, with a full mouth capable of seducing any woman, human or Fae, with its sweet promises. A wide gold band encircled his neck. As boys, their father had given them each an identical torque. Laced with magic, they lent strength to the wearer. The one Hafnar wore he'd wrenched from Lachlan's neck the day he'd brought him to the cavern to suffer eternal damnation. He'd thought Lachlan's more powerful than his own.

Lachlan's gaze raked up and down his brother. Hafnar had kept himself fit and appeared every bit as virile as the day he'd last visited over a century ago. Lachlan had always been the stronger of the two, except when it came to wielding magical powers. A halfling had no chance against a full-blooded Fae except perhaps in physical power and a mind trained to outwit. That hadn't worked out so well for Lachlan given his current quandary.

"I've spent my considerable free time thinking on what cruel bit of fate will befall ye once I'm free of this hell ye've so kindly provided." Lachlan twisted his wrists until the manacles made them bleed. "The revenge I exact will be beyond yer worst nightmare, that I promise ye."

A maniacal smile ignited the fire in Hafnar's eyes. "You don't really think this one wisp of a lass will be different than the others do you? I've watched her, and it was truly a waste of my time. Her skills are uninspiring. It will take little interference from me to ensure her failure. Brenna Sinclair, what the modern world calls a psychologist. It's a term you wouldn't understand of course, but she teaches at a university."

Lachlan swallowed around the lump in his throat and fought to keep any hint of emotion from his face. His eyes narrowed for a moment before he caught himself. Hafnar knew about Brenna. His temper rose at the thought of Hafnar watching her, finding her weaknesses to use against her.

"Ah, yes, I know more about her than you, much more. She has wasted years with wretches like you. Pathetic souls with no strength of mind to endure the hardships life has dealt them, sending out visions asking for help. Some of them have even died. You're not that lucky though, are you? You don't have the choice of whether to live or die. You will live forever. Isn't it grand to be immortal?" Hafnar threw back his head, a hardy laugh seizing him.

"Ye must be a wee bit worried, otherwise ye wouldn't be here. I think the lass has a chance at freeing me, given yer long winded rambling. You mentioned she couldn't save a few, but ye didn't mention the ones she helped. How many of those were there, Hafnar?"

"None. None in the three years since the last one died, and she won't help you either." Hafnar stepped a hair's breadth out of reach of his captive. The tendons in Lachlan's neck strained as he fought to keep the bile from rising to the back of his throat as the sickening sweet breath of his tormentor washed over him.

"Brenna may make it to the shores of the Highlands, but she will never undertake the journey to find you, I'll see to it. You will be just another failure for her, a desperate, pathetic soul she couldn't save. She'll go crawling home defeated and forget you ever existed. And you? You will never leave this place."

"When the lass frees me, ye'd best be prepared to defend yer miserable life. I never wanted Father's crown, but I'll happily burn in hell for killing my own brother before I let ye rule in Father's stead. It can't be worse than what I've endured these past centuries."

Lachlan suspected Hafnar would have killed him long ago if he'd possessed the courage to blatantly disobey the Fae law forbidding interference in the lives of mortals. The Magic would know of the violation and his punishment would be swift and permanent. Lachlan was only half-mortal, but the consequences would be monumental for Hafnar. He'd lose the crown for sure.

"Father thinks you're long dead," Hafnar said.

"Does he now? Then why has he not named ye king? Yer a fool, and Father knows ye're unfit to rule, isn't that the truth of the matter? Brenna will see to it they find me."

"*Never*. She will never come for you."

A moment later, Hafnar was gone.

Lachlan unclenched his fists and lifted his head to the heavens. The overwhelming fear that his brother might be right settled over him. What if Brenna did change her mind about helping him? Would he ever again see a falling star in the vastness of the sky? Would the sun ever thaw his frozen bones? The only thing that kept Lachlan from slipping into madness over the centuries was the one human emotion to which he still clung.

Hope.

###

Brenna was running on empty when she boarded the connecting United flight that would take her from

Liberty Airport to Heathrow. Despite a tearful goodbye to Jen and Merlin, she was excited to be on her way. Although she'd traveled extensively to give talks, she had never traveled to London. She'd have a two-hour layover before continuing to Inverness, which meant she would be able to add a pushpin to the world map hanging in her living room. Layovers definitely counted.

Brenna slid into the window seat of aisle fourteen and crossed her fingers she wouldn't end up sitting next to Chatty Cathy or Conversational Carl. She wanted nothing more than to catch up on a few hours' sleep. Once they were in the air and there was no turning back, she would tell Lachlan she was on her way.

An elderly woman took the middle seat next to Brenna. An attractive young traveling companion assisted the old woman and finished the row. The young man had already procured a pillow and a lap blanket and tucked the aged woman comfortably into her seat.

"I'm Nana Rose. How are you, dear?" the elderly woman said, extending her frail hand to Brenna. "What sort of flyer are you? A talker, a sleeper, or a reader?"

Brenna clasped Nana Rose's hand; a firm grip belied her frail appearance. "I'm Brenna, and I'm a reader on most flights."

"How delightful. So am I. No senseless chatter on this trip, eh?" Nana Rose winked, her position on chatter patently clear. The conversation over, Nana Rose leaned forward, fumbled in the carry-on bag stowed beneath the seat in front of her, and procured a book. Brenna caught a glimpse of the title and stifled a giggle. *Erotic Fairy Tales*.

Brenna waited patiently for the emergency announcement, take off, and the arrival of her mineral water. She downed her drink and closed her eyes. She scrunched down in her seat, cursing the lack of lumbar support, and knew, by the end of the eight hours it took to arrive in London, that she would have a heck of a time standing up straight.

"*Lachlan, can you hear me?*" she thought.

Lachlan didn't react to the sound of her voice. Waist deep in water, he stared intently at the shadows on the cavern wall. Brenna stared as well. Lachlan hung heavily from his manacles. He looked exhausted and Brenna sensed his situation weighed him down mentally and physically.

"*Lachlan, I just wanted to tell you that I'm on my way. I'm about eight hours away from arriving in London. I have a two hour layover, then I'll be on my way to the Highlands.*"

He pulled on his manacles and stood his feet more firmly beneath him. He raised an eyebrow, and a look of surprise etched his features. "I had no idea ye'd be arriving so quickly. That pleases me very much. I've a bit of news to share with ye, lass. It's not good news either. I've had an unwelcome visitor today."

A spark of anger flared in his eyes, and Brenna watched as fresh blood began to ooze at his wrists.

"*You're bleeding.*"

"Aye, well, I tried to wrench the head off me brother's shoulders, but failed in the attempt."

Brenna removed one of the Band-Aids from her wrist and stared down, mesmerized by the fresh cut. She'd been boxing up a semester's worth of folders from her office when she stumbled over her own feet. The folders stacked high in her arms leaned precariously, squeezing them together with her arms to keep them from falling, she only succeeded in giving herself matching folder cuts, one on each wrist. *Keep calm and carry on. Coincidence. Keep calm and carry on.*

"*Go on,*" she said, reaffixing the Band-Aid.

"The man who put me here thought he'd pay me a visit to tell me that he's been watching ye. He doesn't plan to let ye succeed in helping me."

"*Watching me? How can he be watching me? I'm four thousand miles away from you.*"

"Hafnar is a full-blooded Fae prince. He is not a part of the world ye know. He has powers beyond what ye can imagine. If he means to stop yer helping me, then we'll likely run into a snag or two. I can't protect ye."

"*And by that you mean the royal 'we,' you mean me. I'll be facing the wrath of a pissed off Faerie prince who wants you exactly where you are and me out of the picture, is that about right?*"

"Aye. A snag or two."

"*All right. What can he do to stop me? Exactly.*"

"The laws of the Faerie realm prevent him from physically harming ye himself, but he could throw obstacles in yer way that make the journey and the task of helping me dangerous and overwhelming enough that ye simply give up," Lachlan said.

Gooseflesh started at her nape and rippled down her arms. Her heart beat a staccato tune and her mouth went dry. This was not the sort of news that gave one a warm fuzzy feeling.

"So he can't kill me then or slash me with a knife?" she asked.

"That he can't do."

"Well that's a step in the right direction. So, tell me then, what can he do?

"He could cause a horse to fright and ye might be thrown or rent the sky with lightning that strikes a tree near where ye stand. Ye see the difference?"

Brenna dropped her face into her hands and shook her head. Her anxiety was getting the best of her.

"Say something, lass."

Brenna traced the line of her scar with her fingertips.

"Dammit."

"Ye'd best leave now, lass. I know ye don't care much for this part of my day or my night as may be the case," Lachlan said, sobering to the reality of high tide.

Brenna wrung her hands together in her lap. *"I'll stay with you."*

It pained her to watch every wave claw its way up his body. Each upsurge slammed him against the cavern wall at his back, and yet he remained calm. As calm as one could be, knowing that death would win another battle. Lachlan lifted his face to the cavern ceiling, presumably to keep his face above the water for as long as possible.

Brenna inhaled deeply and held her breath until her lungs burned from the effort, and her connection to Lachlan slipped silently into the frigid waters of the Atlantic. Silent tears fell from her eyes and her heart agonized for the man who battled the raging sea and lost. Again.

Nana Rose reached out her liver-spotted hand and touched Brenna's arm. Her twinkling blue eyes seemed to look directly into Brenna's soul.

"Are you all right, my dear?" Nana Rose asked. "You seem a bit out of sorts."

Brenna smiled despite her heavy heart. Nana Rose had seen the tears Brenna shed for Lachlan.

"I'll be fine, Nana Rose. I'm on my way to visit a…friend. He's been going through a rough patch lately, and I'm hoping that I might get him through this difficult time." She offered no more in the way of explanation.

Nana Rose patted Brenna's hand again. "You rest now, dear. You'll need all your strength to help your friend."

Brenna turned and looked out across the vast expanse of ocean, resting her forehead against the coolness of the window. *Dear God, please don't let me fail him.* The last thing she remembered hearing was the voice of a young mother several rows in front of her, singing softly to the infant she held in her arms. She woke to the sound of the captain's voice announcing their descent into Heathrow and the warm touch of Nana Rose's hand still on her arm.

CHAPTER FIVE

Brenna glanced at her watch. Her flight from London to Inverness had landed right on time, and she was on schedule for the drive to MacGregor B&B. She would stop at Lachlan's castle first and see what she could learn. The chili red Mini Cooper she rented sported twin white stripes that spiced up the front and rear styling and contrasted sharply with her faded blue 1984 Land Cruiser at home.

She poked along at first. The whole left hand drive experience unnerved her, but it gave her time to enjoy the land. It was lush and velvet green and promised breathtaking beauty in the later days of summer. Pushing the button to lower the window, she inhaled the scent of damp earth. A sense of peace enfolded her, and her soul sang in delight at the perfection of the moment. She wanted to share it with Lachlan and sent her mind in search of his. He knew the instant she was there and a tentative smile formed on his lips.

"I'm in Scotland, on my way to the Highlands."

"I gave ye difficult news to bear. I thought perhaps, ye'd decided. . ."

"Decided what? Not to help you? I might be scared shitless, thanks to your brother, but I haven't changed my mind. Yet." She inhaled a calming breath.

"I was afraid I'd never see ye again after telling ye of Hafnar."

Brenna gasped at Lachlan's words and the hair on the back of her neck quivered. "Wait, you can see me?"

"Aye, I can. I like to watch ye sleep, lass. It calms me to see ye so peaceful. Though I never met a lass with a pet rat she let sleep in her bed with her."

"A pet r…oh, you mean my Chihuahua. Oh my God, you've been watching me? No one has ever been able to see me, only hear me. Have you seen me naked?"

Lachlan laughed. It was a glorious sound. A full, robust laugh that reverberated in the cavern and echoed in Brenna's heart.

"I'm an honorable man, lass. I've closed my eyes on more than one occasion, though I can't say I haven't seen a bit of flesh. But, on my honor, I look away immediately. It's crossed my mind that the little rat has a good time of it burrowing under the covers with ye." He chuckled to himself and shook his head in amusement.

A blush rose to her cheeks. "I can't believe it. You can actually see me?" She pulled one hand off the steering wheel and covered her scar.

"Don't hide yer scar, lass. Yer beautiful."

She dropped her hand from her face and shook her head in disbelief. Her eyes welled and she fought to keep a tear from spilling down her cheek. “That’s not true, but nice of you to say it anyway.”

He lifted a single eyebrow and cocked his head quizzically. “It is true, lass. Yer hair is the color of a Highland sunset, and yer eyes are like the mist on a rainy morning. Ye’ve fine ivory skin like clotted cream. I could watch you every moment of every day for eternity and never grow tired of yer smile. Ye take my breath away.”

Brenna thought she would puddle on the floorboards with the emotions he evoked. She couldn’t speak. The intensity of his words left little room for conversation.

Moments ticked by. When she recovered herself enough to speak, she said, “Stay with me awhile. We’ll take in the sights, and you can keep me company.”

“I can’t think of anything I’d like more.” His face lit up like she’d offered him the world.

“Good. There’s so much I can show you.”

“How is it that yer moving so fast, and yet I don’t see any horses?” His brow furrowed.

“Well, this is called a car and the horses are under the hood in the form of a combustion engine, which I know absolutely nothing about. I put the key in the ignition and put gas in it every few hundred miles.”

“A few hundred miles ye say? Well, that’s damned convenient. I like that bit of invention. How fast does it go?”

Such a guy question. Brenna pointed at the speedometer. “This gauge tells me I’m going one hundred kilometers per hour. A horse can gallop at a speed of about thirty-eight kilometers per hour.”

“Brenna, Ye should slow down.”

“You’re kidding me. You’re already a back seat driver.” She shook her head and chuckled.

“I’m a what?”

“A back seat driver--it’s a passenger in a car who offers the driver unwanted advice.”

“Ah. So yer poking fun at me because yer going too fast?”

The mini six-speed zagged through an s-curve, the Cooper handling like a dream. The next minute found her slamming on the brakes, swerving off the road and bumping along the shoulder before skidding abruptly to a halt. Thankfully, the airbag remained intact; Brenna rested her forehead against the steering wheel and took a deep breath.

“Shit. You were right.” *I will never live this down.*

A sea of black faces and curving horns stared at her, unmoving and indifferent to her arrival on the scene. The herd of Highland sheep stretched across the entire width of the road and beyond and showed no intention of moving along any time soon.

“Aye. Are ye all right then?”

“Yes. Yes, I’m fine. I, uh, will slow down from here on in I think.”

Determined not to stress over the near miss or the delay, she dug for the camera in her purse. Jen had insisted she take photos to record her adventure in pictures so she wouldn’t forget any details when she recounted her tale. A dozen snapshots later, she honked the horn and maneuvered her way through the mob with no injuries to car or sheep.

After the twenty-minute setback, she continued along the winding road toward her destination. The scenery mesmerized her, and the rhythm of the road soothed her rattled nerves like a lullaby. She kept her word and drove slower, and Lachlan was a model passenger.

The Highlands of Scotland, rich in history, played hideout and home to those whose lives entwined with the glens, and the lochs, and the mountains, a place that would beguile any tortured soul. In another time, under different circumstances, these Highlands would have welcomed her like a long lost love. The hours ticked by without further incident, and her mind stayed connected to the man imprisoned somewhere in this magical land.

"Do you have any idea where you're being held, Lachlan? Do you remember anything from your abduction that might give us a clue to your whereabouts?"

"Nay. I took a blow to the head and woke up chained with the tide coming in. The first time was the worst. But ye never quite get used to drowning."

Brenna's gut clenched. She had to find his family. She had to. "Lachlan, I'm so sorry about what's happened to you. I hope you don't mind, but I'd like to do some thinking."

"Ah. Ye mean without me in yer head? I understand, lass. These last few hours have been a gift I shall never forget. If I never make it out of here, I will always have this day. I thank ye." He bowed his head as if paying homage to her and let go of their connection. She was alone, and a piece of her heart was missing.

Another few hours ticked by. She'd debated the matter but decided she wanted to make her next stop alone. Paying close attention to the GPS, Brenna realized after turning around twice, that no actual road existed to get to Lachlan's castle. Brenna pulled off to the shoulder and parked.

She disconnected the GPS from its cradle and slung her camera around her neck. Up and down undulating hills, she climbed, her strides lengthening at the smell of salt air and seagulls yammering.

The first sight of the castle was majestic. The weathered grey stone rose from the sheer rock face at the edge of a steep shoreline. Surrounded on three sides by the deadly North Sea, she admired Lachlan's choice of a defensible location. The sound of waves pounding the cliffs echoed throughout the surrounding hills. Massive structures stood like sentinels against the sea and sky.

A tall stone archway marked a tunnel that led through the rock. The only obvious entry point to the castle, Brenna walked through, emerged on the other side, and climbed the ancient slabs of stone that formed a stairway. One side of an imposing moss-covered tower loomed over her once she reached the top of the stairs. Crenellated battlements and dozens of arrow slits constructed to stop an enemy before they reached a viable entry to the keep, damning any attackers. The remains of a portcullis stared at her like a gaping maw and led her further into the heart of Lachlan's home.

The first structure she laid her eyes on was a ruinous chapel. Roof long gone and side walls completely demolished, the walls that remained were blackened, perhaps by fire. The second structure might have been the bailey, given its size and location, now reduced to nothing more than an enormous mound of rock. Trepidation, bordering on fear, somersaulted in her stomach. Brenna stood unmoving for long minutes. Curiosity more than courage won out and she shifted her gaze to view the castle proper.

The L-shaped structure stood solemnly, awaiting judgment. A shell of what it had once been, three of the six sides had caved in, taking the interior floors with them in the fall. Soft green moss covered the remains of the once magnificent keep.

Brenna dropped her head and pinched the bridge of her nose. *Dammit. What did I expect?* She'd been right to come here alone.

Climbing over the rubble, she made her way inside. The intact walls were three feet thick and arched windows looked out over the cliff upon which the castle stood, several hundred feet above the North Sea.

Hoisting herself up to sit within the wide arch of a window, she ran her hand along the cool surface of the rock and felt somehow connected to this place, to the time long ago when Lachlan lived here. A massive fireplace stood erect. She could picture him, warm and relaxed in front of it, long legs stretched out, ankles crossed, fine Scotch whisky swirling in a tankard.

She'd spent her life alone. It was only now, after sharing a connection with Lachlan, that she felt lonely. He made her feel things. . .things she didn't understand. The walls she'd spent a lifetime building to protect herself were crumbling. He could be using her and her ability only to free himself. But, he seemed more genuine than desperate. All she knew for sure was that she missed him. Each time their connection severed and they were apart, she longed for his presence.

She had to see him freed. Without his chains and manacles.

Failure was not an option.

Brenna clamored back over the rubble. A faint breeze lifted her hair and blew it across her face, tickling her. The screech of an osprey hovering on a current of air rang through the clamor of the seagulls. A telephoto lens would have come in handy. Sadly, it was at home. With her umbrella.

The long sea grasses that covered the cliff top only sparsely dotted the crumbling rock along the edges. Small round stones hardly larger than pebbles formed the foundation of the entire cliff. Brenna moved to stand at the edge and framed a shot of the imperial raptor.

A sudden *whooshing* rang in her ears and knocked her off balance.

Way off balance.

A precipitous squall of wind hit her from behind. The pudding rock beneath her feet disintegrated and fell away.

And so did she.

She tumbled over the edge and slid down the rocky bluff. When she finally stopped, a good fifty feet from the top, a trickle of blood traced a path from her temple to her jaw then dribbled onto the rocks beneath her. A stream of warmth welled from her knee and flowed down her shin. Climbing back to the top of the cliff proved futile. Every time she moved, more rock crumbled and fell away and she skidded another few feet down.

Wrong direction.

The sea below bided its time and waited to swallow her.

She expected to see her life flash before her eyes, but it didn't. Maybe that was a sign she'd make it out of her precarious situation, though she didn't see how. Not a single twig or branch extended from the cliff. She risked a glance below her, only to be punished by a wave of vertigo. There was no plateau she could maneuver to, just a straight shot into the sea.

The only way off the cliff was suicide.

###

Colin slammed the phone down in its cradle for the fourth time. He'd checked online, her plane landed as scheduled. He checked with two rental car agencies, the second one confirming she rented a red Mini Cooper. The highway authorities had no reports of any mishaps involving Miss Sinclair. The pub in town hadn't seen her and she still wasn't answering her cell phone.

Where the bloody hell is she?

The forty-eight hours since Brenna's call provided plenty of time for Colin to do his research and find out she was never late. She'd been due to arrive hours ago. Out of options, Colin strode to his office door and turned the knob. He hesitated, one last idea crossing his mind. Turning back and flipping through the notes strewn across his desk, he dialed one last number and hoped Jennifer Baker was home.

"Well it's about time you called," said a sleepy voice.

"I'm not her, and she's not here yet," Colin said, his voice terse.

Colin heard fumbling movement on the other end of the line. "You're Colin?"

"Aye, Colin here."

"Let me get my copy of her notes."

Jen muttered to herself, "Final exam schedule, packing list, ah, here it is Scotland itinerary. Flights, rental car, blah blah, the castle. She planned to stop at Lachlan's castle before she checked into your B&B."

"Fuck." Colin slammed the phone down for the fifth time.

He bolted from the room, ran down the hall, pausing at the front door long enough to grab his backpack. It contained a satellite phone, rope, a first aid kit, flashlight, and other assorted sundries. Everything one might need to rescue a damsel in distress. He'd take

Enbarr. The four-wheel drive Cayenne wouldn't get him close enough to the castle to avoid carrying her if she was injured. The license she faxed said a lithe one hundred twenty-five pounds, but women lied and he was in no mood to haul one hundred and fifty plus pounds through the rocks and hills surrounding the castle.

Blasting through the stable door, he ran for Enbarr. The destrier pranced in his stall, agitated. Colin threw a leg over, no saddle, no bridle, no time, and they galloped into the fading light.

CHAPTER SIX

"Breeennnaaa! Where the hell are ye?"

She had no idea how long she'd been clinging to the side of the cliff. The sun was setting, the temperature dropping and she shivered as much from fear as from cold. Numb fingers and toes complicated the task of hanging on for dear life.

"Here…I'm here," she said, her voice barely above a whisper. How he heard her, she couldn't comprehend, but he did.

"Don't move. I'm coming down."

A silhouetted shadow repelled effortlessly down the side of the cliff. He straddled her, reaching around her waist to tie her to him. Panic attacked when he lifted her away from the cliff and into his arms.

"Enbarr, back," he shouted to an unseen ally.

The rope held taut and pulled them, one step at a time, up the steep face of the cliff. Enbarr turned out to be an enormous black stallion. She'd never seen any horse like him. He fit the description of an ancient breed of destrier. No longer holding their weight, he pranced and snorted, but kept his distance from her. Typical male meets psychic reaction.

"Colin? How did you find me?"

"Ye were late. Yer never bloody late, and ye didn't ring Miss Baker when ye should have," he said as he untied the rope. "Ye look like hell, Miss Sinclair."

"Well, I should. I've just been through it."

Colin knelt before her and grabbed the fabric of her ripped jeans at the knee. He wrenched the tear wide open to expose the bloody joint. "I've seen worse," he said and plucked several pebbles from the wound. "Hell of a cut, but it won't need to be stitched."

He eyed the dried blood at her temple and seemed to dismiss the cut as insignificant. "Let's get ye to the manor, so I can get ye cleaned up."

The lack of a saddle coupled with Brenna's exhaustion made the trip to the manor house seem interminable. The sun crept below the horizon but not before Brenna caught her first glimpse of the fortified manor house. It set her heart fluttering in her chest. A glorious building of whitewashed granite with imposing turrets, balustrades, and a double gatehouse, one on either side of the manor entrance. Spring flowers had burst forth from their winter graves in riotous colors. Brilliant yellow daffodils, velvet purple hyacinths, and tiny snowy crocuses along the front of the gatehouses welcomed her.

Colin dismounted and helped Brenna slide from the back of the beast. A gentle smack to the stallion's hindquarter and Enbarr trotted in the direction of the stable where presumably someone would tend him.

Brenna couldn't help but notice Colin towered over her. He stood at least six foot three or four and wore his copper hair cropped short. Powerfully built with broad shoulders and an expansive chest, Brenna averted her gaze before she made a complete fool of herself ogling the man who'd plucked her from certain death. *Thank God he's not wearing a kilt.*

"I've fixed a room for ye. It's got the best views of the property, though I hope you can manage the stairs to get there," he said, pointing to the top floor of the tower. The manor itself stood two stories, but the tower stood taller at three stories.

Brenna looked down at the bloody mess that was her knee and cringed at the long climb. She hobbled through the front door Colin held open for her and gimped into the manor's great hall. It was breathtaking. The floor was a rich golden pine. Years of use had given it an undulating, smooth texture. Whitewashed stone walls soared above them. Tremendous wooden beams bridged the expanse overhead and held the weight of the floor above. Intricately woven tapestries hung throughout the room; no doubt they took someone a lifetime to complete. The largest one hung directly centered above the head of the great hall table and drew Brenna's gaze.

She stared at the weaving. The woman rode a horse that looked like Enbarr. But more disturbing was the woman's face. She swallowed hard and reached out toward the material.

"Rather a shock for ye I imagine," Colin said.

Brenna turned to him her mouth agape. "Yes, second one today, actually."

"Come, let's get ye cleaned up and settled in yer room. There'll be time later to answer yer questions," Colin said.

The weaving appeared old. Very old. The colors were faded, muted like a Monet. Castle MacGregor was depicted in the background of the scene. A dragon circled high above the turrets, and upon the back of a black stallion, a rider, who could only be Lachlan. Seated on the stallion in front of Lachlan was a woman, who could only be her.

"Oh no, I'm not going anywhere until we talk about that tapestry." She limped to the great hall table, pulled out a massive oak chair and plopped herself down.

"I can see ye won't be wasting any time with pleasantries, will ye now?" he said with a chuckle. He joined her at the table and removed the first aid kit from the backpack he carried. "The tapestry arrived at Lachlan's castle shortly after his disappearance. No one can say who made it, only that there is magic in the warp and weft of the weave. It didn't have your likeness in it when it first arrived. It was thought simply to be a kindly remembrance of the man so many respected and loved."

Colin used his bare hands to rip her torn jean leg completely off above her wounded knee, then he produced a set of tweezers from the first aid kit and plucked bits of gravel from the wound.

"It was two hundred years before the tapestry changed for the first time. It portends the future, ye see. It tells us that someone will be coming to make the journey to free Lachlan. Yer likeness is the third one to appear."

"The third? Lachlan mentioned one, but not two. What happened to them?"

"Yes. Well, the first one decided she didn't have the skill or the courage or some such that it took to help the lad. The second one met with an untimely demise. Their images disappeared from the tapestry shortly after they departed. The last one, almost a hundred years ago."

Colin broke out a bottle of something or other and twisted off the cap to douse her wound with it. Brenna scooted back in her chair and held her breath, expecting the liquid to sting.

"I asked ye to fax me your license the day we spoke on the phone, so I could see if ye were the lass whose likeness appeared in the tapestry a few weeks before ye called. When I knew it was ye, I'd have given ye all I have just to get ye this far, Miss Sinclair. I can't imagine Lachlan could stand for another of ye to abandon him. He's waited six centuries for ye."

Six centuries.

Like a white hot blade, the thought of Lachlan suffering for six centuries pierced her to the core. She'd never asked how long Lachlan had been held captive. Brenna felt a tingle that started at her temples and skittered downward, her blood draining to pool in her feet. She was going to throw up or pass out, she didn't know which.

Colin slathered an ointment on her knee and wrapped it with a gauze and white tape. Chair legs scraped the wood floor as Colin pulled out a chair and seated himself to face her. He leaned forward, rested his elbows on his knees, and watched as she paled.

"I think I'm going to be—"

"Ye'll do no such thing," Colin said.

She felt as though a hand had closed around her throat. "I promised Lachlan that I would try to find his father or sister and let them know of his captivity. I can't possibly rescue him myself. I shouldn't be in the tapestry at all."

"It's not that simple, Miss Sinclair. Nobody knew what happened to Lachlan. He rode out one morning to check on his tenants and never returned. Search parties combed the Highlands for months. Lachlan's father and sister, King Ratava of the Fae and Princess Ariel, arrived several weeks into the search. Every Fae joined in the hunt for him in their realm and in ours. It was years before they stopped scouring the lands.

"The first lass who appeared in the tapestry told us Lachlan was a captive. The second lass told us who held him, but by then his father and sister had long since left our realm and returned to theirs. There was no one to stop Hafnar. By the time the first lass appeared, King Ratava had already sealed the passages between our worlds. The king wanted no reminder of the mortal world that brought him such grief. We've not been able to get word to him that Lachlan is alive. It's been the duty of every clan historian to find his family and tell them he lives. Not one of us has succeeded. Instead, we've made a plan for ye."

"A plan? What plan?"

"When the women started showing up in the tapestry we made a plan. The only part missing has been you. Now that yer here, we can begin."

"I didn't sign on for this, Colin. I…no, I can't," Brenna stammered, her mind racing with fear.

"The tapestry doesn't lie."

"Yes, it does. Two other women were chosen and they failed. I'm not here to rescue him."

"But ye are. The magic has chosen ye. Ye can see him, ye can hear him, and ye crossed the Atlantic to get this far. Yer fate has brought ye here. Now ye must have faith ye can save him."

Time ceased to exist as Brenna stared at the tapestry. She looked radiant. So much so that one might overlook the slash marring her cheek. A glow from within sang of joy and contentment, a soothing, comforting song. She didn't think she had ever looked as happy as she did in that tapestry sitting astride the black stallion, Lachlan's arms wrapped tightly around her waist. Could she really be that happy? Was this really her destiny, the reason she'd been cursed with visions?

"Come. Let's get ye settled in yer room."

The circular staircase wound round and round. Colin climbed it effortlessly; she lagged behind, her swollen knee impeding her progress. He pushed opened the stout oak door and waited for her to catch up and precede him into the room.

The bed rested on a raised dais in the center of the room. Four massive posts, one at each corner held rich burgundy draperies that she could close to keep out the draft, the light, and her nightmares. The bed was easily ten feet wide and could sleep a family of five if so inclined. A chocolate colored faux mink throw draped invitingly across the foot of it and Brenna ran her hand over the fake fur. It tickled her palm, sending little jolts of pleasure running up her arm.

"This is my room?" Brenna asked, uncertain.

"Aye, it is." Colin said, his hands straying to his hips defensively.

"I've never seen a more perfect room. It's straight out of a fairy tale. Give me an Internet connection and I could stay here forever," she said.

"Wi-Fi via satellite uplink, no extra charge," Colin said.

The room easily measured forty feet in diameter with stained glass windows set into the thick stone walls every few feet around the circumference. The windows were tall and arched at the top. Wide stone sills were low enough that Merlin, who stood an imposing six inches off the ground, could easily access them to sun himself. She already missed her little guy.

An assortment of lusciously thick, jewel-toned carpets lay strewn across the stone floor. She planted herself at the edge of the bed and yanked off her boots, tossing them callously out of the way and burrowed her toes into the nearest carpet like a worm boring into an apple.

"Lachlan's ruined castle tower was recreated here, at this manor house, after the original MacGregor castle fell into ruin. The bed was hand carved by the laird himself. It was missing for several centuries but came up for auction at Sotheby's some years ago, and I was contacted. Lachlan carved his name, see here, and the auction folks thought there might be some family interest," Colin said, indicating the carved signature. "Cost me a bloody fortune."

Brenna ran her fingers over the name, Lachlan Alexander Stuart MacGregor, 1394. The bed had been carved over six hundred years ago by the man who sought her help. Roses swirled on their vines, intricately carved into the surface; she could imagine the sun streaming through the stained glass windows coaxing the inside garden to flourish with blooms. The wood was still warm to her touch from the rays of the late afternoon sun.

He canted his head to the left. "Through that door are all the modern conveniences of a bathroom. Get yerself a hot bath, but keep that knee dry. There's a shirt and sweatpants in the wardrobe there," he said, pointing the way. "We'll retrieve yer car and luggage tomorrow. I'll be back in an hour with supper and we'll talk some more."

A heavy breath puffed from her mouth and her bangs fluttered from the exhalation. She cast him a sidelong glance. "I told Lachlan I would help find his family, but I can't do that can I? You just told me that every clan historian has been tasked with doing exactly that, but none of you has succeeded in doing so, because the portals are sealed." She searched his eyes for the answer.

"Aye, Miss Sinclair. Ye've figured out the truth of it. Now try to relax some. I'll be back soon with yer supper."

Long strides carried him from the room. The echo of the door latch falling into place signaled she was alone with her thoughts.

Brenna meant to take a long soak in the tub and change out of her torn, filthy clothes. But it was easier to just lay back on the feathered bed and dream about hot streaming water washing away the day.

###

Darkness seeped in from the windows, her first hint that she had slept longer than she intended. The soft flicker of a flame from a candle on her nightstand and a low fire burning in the massive fireplace told her Colin had come and gone without disturbing her. A tray with a carafe of wine, bread, and cheese rested on the nightstand keeping vigil with the candle. Her stomach growled loudly, and she threw off the blanket Colin had used to cover her.

She tested her weight on her injured knee and found it held. She took the food-laden tray and settled closer to the fire. "Lachlan, are you there?"

"I'm here, lass. Did ye think I'd escaped?" he asked with a hint of mischief in his voice.

"Sorry, I knew you were there, I guess it was just my way of asking if I could talk with you awhile."

"Aye, lass, yer voice is a welcome reprieve from the incessant sound of the waves. I think when I leave this place, I'll not be interested in hearing the ocean waters ever again. Have ye found my castle, Brenna? I think ye must have; there can only be one bed carved in the manner as the one in that bed chamber." He gazed over her shoulder at the massive four-poster.

It unsettled her the way he could see her. Running a hand through her hair, she combed it with her fingers. Positive her makeup had slid off her face hours ago, she regretted not taking a few minutes to freshen up before laying down to rest.

"What happened to ye, Brenna? A black eye, is that what I see?" He squinted to get a better look at her and his hands fisted.

"I've good news and bad news, Lachlan, which do you want to hear first?"

"I want to hear why the hell yer injured; right now, let's have it."

"I found your castle. It's several miles from here. It isn't as you remember it, Lachlan. A lot of time has passed since you were last there. I don't know the details of how it happened, but the castle is no longer standing. There are parts of it that remain, but it's…it's fallen into ruins. I'm sorry. This room was built in the likeness of the original, that's why it seems so familiar to you."

Brenna held her breath, waiting for his reaction to the news. She had dreaded the moment she would have to tell him. Now that moment was over, and she realized that she had spent so much time worrying about telling him, she'd not thought how he would react to the news.

"Well, I'm taking that was the good news," was his calm reply. He dropped his gaze to the cavern floor, shaking his head. "I was wrong to think it would have survived after so long, but somehow, I had hoped. Now, how did ye get that eye blackened?"

"Actually, that was the bad news."

His eyes narrowed speculatively. "I'm not certain I agree with yer meaning."

"I think it was just a blast of wind. I don't know. I was near the edge of the cliff, taking pictures, when a gust threw me off balance and I fell over the edge. I slid a ways, bounced around a heck of a lot, and tore up my knee a bit. I guess I got a black eye, too. I'm fine now, just bruised and sore."

"Hrmph. And I suppose ye think it was an accident, that wind? I don't suppose it occurred to ye that Hafnar conjured that wind purposefully to deter yer efforts to help me?"

Brenna's last nerve, frayed and worn, snapped. She gathered herself and stood. Wishing she were taller, she shifted her weight to her good knee and placed one hand on her hip.

"Of course I thought of that, right after I fell and was hanging on for my damn life. I'm not stupid, Lachlan. I'm just not used to having a fricking faerie follow me around trying to kill me, but don't worry. I'm a quick study. I get it." Her hand gestured wildly to punctuate her words.

Silence pervaded the cavern. Lachlan alternated between flexing and fisting his hands, a tick quivered along his jaw line. "I'm sorry, lass, but ye don't 'get it' as ye say. Each day I'm resigned to a death sentence at the hands of my brother. Twice a day the sea takes my life, and I am so cold it feels like bits of glass running in my veins, but that's nothing, nothing, as painful as fearing for yer safety. I know better than anyone what Hafnar is capable of. If I were free, I wouldn't let anything harm ye. Ever. But right now, I can't protect ye. I can't keep ye safe. That, truly kills me, lass. I wish ye'd have reached for me when ye fell. Maybe the least I could have done is brought ye a bit of comfort."

"It doesn't matter, now. It's over. I'm fine," Brenna reassured him.

Lachlan's chin dropped to his chest and long seconds ticked by before he spoke again. "I'll take the other news, if ye please."

A tiny tendril of hope, that he might care about her beyond her promise to help him find his family, took root in her chest, right beside her heart. He cared about her, worried over her safety. Unfortunately, she'd have to break that promise. With the passages between Faerie and her world sealed, there was no chance of finding his family. It was too soon to tell him. Maybe. Just maybe she and Colin would find a way.

"It seems Colin MacGregor has a plan to help us."

A spark lit in the depths of Lachlan's emerald eyes. A tentative smile broke across his face, and her heart palpitated in her chest. She felt like a mousey sixteen-year-old caught looking at the football quarterback. She turned her gaze away from him and hoped the redness she could feel flushing her cheeks would go unnoticed.

"Aye, that is good news. Though, I worry the remainder of the journey will only grow more treacherous."

Brenna got up to grab the throw to lay it before the fire. "Would you like to see your castle tomorrow?" she asked, changing the subject. "There's a stable on the estate here, I'll see if Colin will ride there with me in the morning."

His gaze lingered. "Aye, lass, I'd like that."

Brenna poured herself another glass of wine and stared into the fire. The flames drew her in, washing her with warmth and peace, two things Lachlan had lived without for a very long time. Her last nerve mended itself, and she decided tomorrow would arrive soon enough, so she stopped fretting over what it held. Colin would tell her what he could, and then at least the wondering would be over.

"Will you stay with me until I fall asleep?"

"Aye, lass. I always do, whether ye know it or not."

Brenna curled up by the fire with her blanket and wished it was the man who shared her mind. Perhaps one day, it would be.

CHAPTER SEVEN

Brilliant colored light danced with the rising sun and streamed through the stained glass windows into Brenna's room. A glance at her watch confirmed it was nearly eleven thirty in the morning, proof positive she was not a morning person. She sat up from her slumbering spot by the hearth. A splash of red caught her eye, and she stood up slowly, wincing as each muscle screamed against the effort. Colin had retrieved her luggage and set it just inside her room. Correction. Jen's luggage. Brenna would never have picked out red Dior that sported exquisite taste, but shouted overpriced and proud of it.

Her subconscious must have ruminated through the night because Brenna woke with a list of questions for Colin. Shuffling stiffly over to her jam-packed carry-on bag, she pulled out the blank notebooks she'd brought with her, selecting the one with the purple cover along with a matching purple pen. It didn't matter if her shirts were wrinkled, or her socks didn't match, or that her jackets and sweaters were covered in dog fur, but it did matter that the ink color matched the cover of the notebook. Five minutes and copious notes later, she headed for a long, hot shower. Then washed, dressed, and ready to face the day, she descended the stairs, round and round. The shower had warmed her muscles and the exercise helped work out the kinks.

Colin sat at the immense oak table in the great hall, coffee and pastry set out before him. "Good morning," he said with a wide smile on his face. "How's that knee doing?"

"A little better I guess. I'm sure it'll be killing me by the end of the day. Thanks for leaving me something to eat. I woke up starving in the middle of the night."

"Have some breakfast," he said, canting his head toward the plate of pastries. "I know ye've a sweet tooth. I checked."

"You've checked, huh? You said a similar thing yesterday. You knew I was never late because you'd 'checked.' How exactly have you done that? And why? Am I under some kind of investigation or something?" She poured herself a cup of coffee from the sideboard and grabbed a couple of turnovers from the silver serving tray. She sat in the chair across from Colin and waited for him to enlighten her.

"Aye. I did look into yer background. I told ye that when ye called that I would see what ye were about. Lucky for Lachlan, ye passed the test."

"Well, had I known, I might have studied, but that doesn't tell me why you checked up on me or how?"

"We don't know who made the tapestry or why. Could be Hafnar himself created the thing as some depraved joke. If that were so, the magic might choose one who would harm Lachlan, or kill him, leaving Hafnar's hands unsoiled."

A bite of croissant slipped down the wrong pipe, and Brenna coughed violently to dislodge the offending lump. How could he possibly think she would ever hurt Lachlan?

"As to the how, let's just say I have friends in low places with whom I exchange money for information."

"Hmm. I hope I didn't cost you too much?"

Colin smiled at her sarcasm.

"I spoke with Lachlan last night. I told him that his castle hadn't survived the years he's been gone. Can we ride out to the site this afternoon and show him what remains of it?"

Colin pushed his chair away from the table. "Let's pack some food for lunch and then we can be on our way. It's probably time ye were properly introduced to Enbarr," Colin said. "It'll be him that leads ye to Lachlan. Best if ye learn to ride the beast before ye start the journey. He's not like those stable ponies yer used to riding."

Brenna bristled at Colin's words, closed her notebook, threaded the purple pen through the spine, and followed him to the kitchen. The man certainly made assumptions, but she'd disabuse him of those later, after she'd learned more.

Lunch took only minutes to pack, and then they headed out a rear entrance toward the stable. Solidly built of stone, the stable foundation rose several feet before giving way to the walls and ceiling of native Scotch pine. Open shutters let in the late morning light, and dust motes floated, silver and shimmering, like snowflakes suspended from invisible threads.

Brenna shivered, partly from excitement, partly from the cool air. Enough stalls to hold a small infantry of horses extended the length of the stable along both sides. Brenna counted only three inhabitants of the massive space as they made their way to the far end of the building.

"Grab an apple from our lunch bag, Miss Sinclair, and see if ye can make friends with the black beast, there," he pointed to the last stall, "and I'll get Sidra saddled up for the ride. I'll be along in a minute to saddle him as well."

Brenna headed for Enbarr, who eyed her with interest as she approached. He whinnied loudly and blew air heavily from his nostrils. It was clear he caught sight of the apple when he stomped his front feet and high stepped around his stall. Hanging his enormous black head over the side of the railing, he nodded vigorously in silent demand for the sweet treat.

Brenna approached him with caution. She was an experienced rider, but he was immense. Twenty-four hands at least. His muscles rippled across his fore and hindquarters, and restrained power emanated off him in waves. The beast had obsidian eyes bright with intelligence and an iridescent black coat that shimmered with blue light. The similarity between Enbarr and the destrier in the tapestry was striking.

Enbarr greedily curled his lips back and stretched his neck to take the apple from her. One loud crunch, a bit of apple spray, and it vanished. Enbarr smelled her hair and when she stepped closer, he nuzzled her neck and snorted in her ear. Pawing the ground restlessly, he awaited his saddle. She soothed him with whispered endearments.

"Looks like the two of ye will be getting on just fine," Colin said as he walked up next to her.

"You know, I haven't properly thanked you for what you did yesterday. I really thought that fall was going to be the end of me. Thank you for saving me."

The hard lines at the corners of his mouth softened for a fraction of a second. "I'll get him saddled today, but ye'll be needing to practice yerself tomorrow," he said, ignoring her acknowledgment of his rescue.

"I'm not worried about saddling him, not much anyway, I'm worried about being able to mount him," she said.

"Aye, he's quite a beast. He has a trick to show ye, don't ye, Enbarr?" he asked, turning his attention to the stallion.

Colin finished getting Enbarr ready while Brenna fed him a handful of alfalfa. Colin led him out of his stall and gave him a command to mount. Enbarr gracefully bent down on one knee allowing Brenna to hop on his back, despite her pained muscles and injured parts. As soon as she was settled and held the reins, he rose to all fours with the grace of a fine courtly gentleman.

"I love that trick, Colin. Did you teach him that?" Brenna asked.

"No, Miss Sinclair, Lachlan himself is responsible for that bit of work."

"Lachlan?" Brenna said, her brows drawn together with a look of consternation. "How can that be? Lachlan's been gone for six hundred years." She stared at Colin for several long beats. "You can't mean that Enbarr is…is immortal too?"

"Aye, he is. He once belonged to an ancient sea god. He can travel farther and faster than any beast ye'll ever ride, unless of course ye find yerself on the back of a dragon."

"You know, Colin, I'm having a hard enough time believing that Lachlan and Enbarr are immortal. I wouldn't even believe that except I've seen with my own eyes that Lachlan recovers from drowning at every high tide; but if you think I believe there are dragons, you've lost your mind," she said with an edge to her voice, eyebrows furrowed.

Colin chuckled. "Believe what ye will."

She shifted the reins to one hand, freeing the other to rest haughtily on her hip a flash of temper rising to her face.

"Let's get going." Dragons my ass.

Colin led them down the gravel drive and across the road to a well-worn path. Brenna let the silence settle over her and breathed deeply of the moist, heavy air. The sun shone, but rain hung threateningly and low clouds blurred the horizon. The land was hilly and covered with spring grass and patches of tiny blooming yellow flowers. She looked at the surroundings through which they rode, and passion for the land unfurled in her soul.

"Ye'll never be the same once you lose yer heart to the Highlands," Colin said, seeming to read her thoughts. "And ye will."

"You're not psychic, or immortal, or part Fae, are you. Colin?"

A wide grin split his face. "I'm a man with a duty handed down to me by the generations that preceded me. Though I've often wondered at the glories of the Fae realm."

“What do you know of Faerie?” They passed the time with idle chatter until the horses trotted side by side through the stone tunnel, then the portcullis to the grounds of the ruined castle.

“I thought at first it was a good idea for Lachlan to see the remains of his castle, but now that we’re here, I’m not so sure,” Brenna said.

“Ye gave him the choice. If he didn't want to see, he would have told ye so,” Colin said. “Ye’re his eyes, lass. Ye need only let him see. Ye needn’t say anything. Ye need to give him a bit more credit. He’s lost more than his castle these past years.”

Brenna nodded her agreement and was thankful that Colin displayed a greater wisdom than she possessed right now. She had found an ally. The psychic abilities she endured separated her from society as effectively as a physical disability or a mental handicap. She had never fit in, but here, so far from home, a stranger had accepted her, psychic disability and all.

“I can see the wheels turning. What is it?” Colin asked.

“I was thinking how you didn’t even flinch when you learned I had visions.”

Colin laughed heartily and slapped his hand on his knee. “I believe in faeries, immortals, dragons, and a whole host of other creatures, and ye think it odd I’d believe ye have visions? Ah, yer amusing, but no more unusual around these parts than being born with blue eyes.”

“Right. Blue eyes and psychic. Nothing unusual about that,” Brenna muttered. “Let’s start with the chapel. Ready?”

Colin nodded, his outburst of laughter gone, his stoic countenance restored. Brenna swung her leg over the saddle and dismounted with the grace of a portly rhino. She skewed her face and with a groan handed over Enbarr's reins. Her knee already ached.

Her mind reached for Lachlan. "Good morning," she said aloud, so Colin could follow at least half of the conversation. She made herself sound cheerful and slapped a smile on her face, hoping her feigned demeanor would reassure Lachlan.

"Ah, lass, 'tis good to see ye. Ye slept a bit fitfully last evening. Worried about this morning I imagine. Pay me no mind, lass. Let's see what ye've got to show me," Lachlan said. He seemed perfectly calm and collected, which gave her the extra bit of strength she needed.

Colin walked up behind her and she turned to face him. "Lachlan, this is Colin. He's the man I've been telling you about; the one who rescued me from the side of the cliff yesterday."

Lachlan cocked an eyebrow and gave Colin a once over glare. "Are ye sure about him, lass? He looks a bit priggish if ye ask me."

Brenna gasped, surprised by the comment. "Ah, well. You've only just met him. I can assure you, that's not the case."

Colin refrained from asking about the exchange, and they simply began to walk. The three of them tenuously connected in their silence, no words needed to bind them in their task.

"Does Colin know how long the castle has been in ruins?" Lachlan asked.

Brenna relayed the question to Colin.

"From what I know from earlier clan historians it was attacked shortly after ye disappeared," Colin said. "Search parties scoured the Highlands looking for ye. Only a handful of yer men stayed behind to guard the castle, most of them young and unseasoned. The damage was severe. During one attack, a handful of men forced the servants into the chapel, barred the doors, and torched the roof. A young boy, who'd hidden in the garderobe waited for the men to ride out and opened the barred doors before anyone perished."

"Can you hear all of this Lachlan?" Brenna asked.

"Aye, lass. What ye can hear, I can too. I just don't like the sound of torment."

Brenna shoved her hands in her pockets and nodded at Colin to continue.

"The damage could have been repaired in time, but whoever led the attacks came back again and again and in the end, yer people abandoned it in fear for their lives. With nobody to defend or occupy yer home, time was unkind to what remained."

"Hafnar. I have no enemies other than him. I imagine it was he and his cronies that carried out the attacks. I can't blame the servants for leaving, nor my family. I wasn't there for them when they needed me," Lachlan said.

The planes of his face hardened, muscles taught with emotion. A brief battle with the manacles ensued. "I can't even hit anything." His voice shook with anger. "Leave me awhile, lass." His eyes pleaded for understanding.

CHAPTER EIGHT

Brenna refused to step within fifty feet of the precipitous cliff that nearly claimed her life the day before. It wasn't the cliff she feared, but Hafnar. His hatred ran rampant. Power fueled by vengeance formed a deadly combination. Just the thought of him made her arms break out in gooseflesh.

Even from a safe distance, she saw the spray from the waves below reach for the sky above, yearning to be a part of it. The smell of salt tinged the air. She found it refreshing. Lachlan, she suspected, found it oppressive.

The ruined chapel beckoned her to step within its hallowed walls. What remained of them anyway. A premonition, perhaps, that the God her parents had beseeched for help when she had her psychic episodes might lend protection from Hafnar. She hoped he would rot in hell. Was there a hell for faeries? She supposed not. Being immortal, he would escape such a fate. A fleeting moment of guilt for her evil thoughts in a house of God caught her unaware. Brenna pushed the feeling aside.

Colin joined her in the chapel. He settled himself on a stone stair that lead from the nave to the altar and motioned for her to join him.

An impulsive urge to run screaming from the church before Colin could utter a word unbalanced her. She steeled herself against the compulsion and sat clumsily next to him, her injured leg splayed out before her. "You're not going to start with 'once upon a time' are you?"

The curve of his mouth hinted at a smile. "Nay, but I'm not exactly sure of the right place to begin."

"Well, then, I'll start." She flipped open the purple cover of her notebook and slipped the matching pen from its spine. "Why am I the one who's been chosen to find Lachlan? Isn't there someone better suited for this undertaking?"

"The magic in the tapestry has chosen ye. I can't say why. But who better suited for the task than one who shares a connection with the man? The other two lasses had yer psychic ability as well, so I'm guessing that's the fundamental reason the magic found ye. And I can tell ye, yer the last chance he has to gain his freedom."

"How do you know that? There were two who came before me. One could logically conclude there will be more who follow."

"We're not talking about logic. We're talking about magic." He reached inside his jacket pocket and removed a leather bound book. "This diary was found long after the two lasses came and went. It's the journal of a man who was present when Lachlan was abducted.

He may have even been involved, though he doesn't say in his journal. He does say that in addition to being held prisoner, Lachlan is bound by a spell cast by Hafnar. Lachlan knows nothing of this spell. It will be yer choice to tell him or not."

Colin handed her the journal. The worn leather was thin in spots but in remarkably fine condition. The thin parchment pages whispered a pleasant sound when she turned them.

"It looks like it's written in Middle English. Can you read it?"

"Sadly, no. But I've had it interpreted."

"What does it say about the spell?" she asked, relinquishing the book into his hands.

"It says there shall only be three who can find him, and should they fail, the immortal blood in his veins shall cease. If that happens, he will become mortal and the tide will take him one last time."

Oh my God. I am the third.

She shook the thought from her. "How am I going to do this? I'm a professor at a university. I don't have the skills to find Lachlan."

"Ye can, and ye will, and I'll help ye. Ye must use yer gift to relieve his suffering."

Colin cocked an eyebrow and waited for her response. Brenna tossed the notebook onto the stone floor then dropped her forehead into her hands and huffed in frustration.

"What if I fail? How am I supposed to live with myself if I fail again?"

Slivers of cold from the stone floor pricked her. Unable to sit still any longer, she rose and limped from one end of the nave to the other, turned, and retraced her steps.

"If ye don't undertake the task, ye've already failed, don't ye see that? How will ye live with that, Miss Sinclair?"

"Miserably, that's how. Someone has already died because of me. Do you have any idea what that feels like? Do you know the pain of having your heart hacked out of your chest and your soul shredded to bits? It's a son-of-a-bitch; and so are you, asking this of me."

The feral glint in his eyes burned brighter. "I've been there and survived, so don't think ye can outdo me with yer past. Lachlan suffers a fate worse than death, don't ye agree? Ye'll never forgive yerself if ye don't try."

She held out her hand in Colin's direction, palm facing out in the American "talk to the hand" vernacular.

Colin pursed his lips, forming a harsh line across his face. "All right. Let's take a break."

Brenna noticed the sun had already passed its zenith and headed on its downward descent. It would be hours yet before the watercolors of the gloaming would paint the sky. Colin rose from the ruined chapel and whistled softly for Sidra. The snow white mare trotted over to Colin, and he removed their lunch from her saddlebag. Silence descended, and Brenna took advantage of the opportunity to digest the details she had learned.

"Tell me more about the portals to Faerie. Are you absolutely sure they are sealed? Maybe there is a back door or a secret passage of some sort?"

"Nay, Miss Sinclair. There is not. When the portals were closed, several fae were stranded here in our realm. They've tried every means within their power to return home, but to no avail."

So much for that idea.

"Well then, I guess you'd better lay out the plan you've devised." Brenna polished off the rest of her sandwich then purposefully sat on her hands to keep her palm from glaring at him.

"Mannin Mac Lir, have ye heard of him?"

Brenna shook her head.

"He was the ancient Celtic god of the sea and indebted to the MacGregor clan for their assistance in a long ago battle. He gifted them four relics of immeasurable value. The first was The Answerer, a great sword that can cut through flesh like butter, creating wounds no healer could hope to cure. The second was a cloak woven by the powers of the Tuatha De Danaan that shields the wearer from all eyes, both Fae and human, so that they are invisible. The third is a breast plate which no weapon can ever pierce, and the fourth, is Enbarr."

"So you have Enbarr, but where are the other items?"

Colin lifted an eyebrow and a smile tugged at his mouth. "We have them all but one, the breastplate. When I knew ye were coming, I reinitiated my search for that piece. The MacKenzie clan stole it from us three hundred years ago or so. I've gotten a few leads in the past week, but so far, none of them have panned out. The other relics are well hidden and safe."

"So what does possession of these things have to do with your plan? We're not telling ghost stories around a campfire here, Colin. Spit it out." A flush of heat born of annoyance tinged her cheeks. Her patience was stretched thin.

"There is a connection between Enbarr and the tapestry. A magic binds them. He will only bear the women in the tapestry to Lachlan. So Enbarr will lead you to Lachlan. The cloak will hide you from danger, and the Answerer will cut through the magic of the chains that hold Lachlan prisoner. When I locate the breastplate, it will keep yer body protected. No weapon can penetrate it."

"That's it? That's the plan? You're joking?" Brenna heaved herself off the ground, slapped her hand onto her hip and glared, waiting for him to say more. He didn't. "God help me, you're not joking. That's it then? That's everything you know?"

"Aye."

Brenna paced several lengths of the chapel then clucked softly in the way she did to call Merlin to her. Heightened hearing brought Enbarr trotting to her side, nuzzling her hand, hoping for another apple, he found it empty.

"Mount, Enbarr," she commanded in a voice much stronger than she felt. The obedient stallion knelt down for her to mount his broad back.

She settled in the saddle and leaned forward stroking his neck. "Let's go home," she whispered. Enbarr led the way, and Colin and Sidra scrambled to bring up the rear of the party of two. The wind picked up, and the air was heavy with moisture when they were still several miles from the manor house.

Colin suggested that they pick up the pace before the downpour started, and Brenna tucked low on Enbarr's back, touching him lightly with her heels. That small gesture was all it took for him to stretch long and low, head down, until he ran faster than a falling raindrop. Brenna was stunned with the speed at which they moved, every pounding stride strong and sure. Any thought that Enbarr might be just an ordinary stallion vanished with her next heartbeat.

Brenna scanned the ground in front of them, a second pair of eyes watching for danger along their flight path. A small mound of rocks protruded just at the edge of their intended course. She cringed, hoping the beast wouldn't stumble. In an instant, Enbarr adjusted his stride and direction to avoid the outcropping of rocks by a slight margin. To their left, a clump of newly blossoming yellow flowers, Brenna looked slightly right and the flowers remained untouched. A tickle of bewilderment brought gooseflesh creeping across her chest. Swiftly moving stallions don't avoid patches of new blooms.

Again, this time she looked left. Enbarr followed her silent command without fail. Brenna called Enbarr to a halt with her mind.

Holy shit!

She slid her leg over Enbarr's back and dropped to the ground, her weight on her good leg. A thrill of excitement made her shiver and her blood pressure swung up a few millimeters of mercury. She stepped away thinking distance would break the connection. The night Colin rescued her, he used the command 'back.' She issued the directive with a thought, and he obeyed.

Holy shit!

The muffled sound of hooves caught her attention. Sidra's sides heaved like a bellows from her effort to catch up.

"What is it? What's wrong?"

"Did you…I can…how did…"

"Bloody hell." Colin dismounted and closed the distance to Brenna in a few easy strides. He grabbed her shoulders and turned her to face him. "Are ye hurt?"

"I can control him, Colin. Enbarr, I can communicate with him through my thoughts. Did you know that would happen?" she asked.

He let go of her shoulders and raked a hand through his hair, breathing out a heavy sigh. "I know Lachlan shared this same connection with Enbarr," he replied. "Perhaps with a connection to the both of ye is how he'll be taking ye to the cavern where Lachlan is held. That makes rather a lot of sense, don't ye think?"

Dumbfounded with this new development, she nodded reflexively in answer to the question. "Mount," she thought and Enbarr reacted to the command exactly as Lachlan had taught him. She mounted the steed and without moving a muscle, she called to mind a simple image of the manor stable. Enbarr turned around and headed directly for his stall and a dinner of oats. Her thought of a perfectly ripe, sweet apple had him at a flat out run for the distance left to cover before they reached home.

"Why do I think this is home, Enbarr?" she said as the beast headed for the shelter of the stable. Fat, heavy raindrops fell from the sky just as Enbarr slowed his pace for the last few yards to the open barn door. Brenna dismounted and turned to await the arrival of Colin and Sidra.

"I'll get you your apple, my friend."

###

Brenna ignored the tapestry in the great hall as she passed. Several flights of stairs loomed ahead of her. Sore muscles strung taut as harp strings sang a song of lament as she hobbled up the steps, feeling decrepit and listless. Her emotions ran the gamut from elation over the connection she shared with Enbarr, to distressed over the plan MacGregor clan historians had concocted through the centuries. It was a ridiculous plan. She wasn't a warrior; she was a psychic freak. What Colin asked of her was suicide. Hafnar would surely see her dead through some twisted stunt. Colin should have just left her hanging onto the side of the cliff that first night.

Brenna shut the bedroom door behind her and leaned against it, closing her eyes. Today had to be one of the most bizarre days of her life. Two chairs flanked a small writing desk. She swiped a pillow from the massive four-poster, tossed it onto one of the chairs, and placed her leg on the pillow than sat down in the other chair. Her knee throbbed from too much use too soon. If it weren't a thousand miles to the kitchen, she'd get herself an ice pack.

Instead, she flipped open her laptop and composed an email to Jen. She thought it best to leave out some of the details. No need to trouble her when she could worry enough for the both of them.

"Miss Sinclair, are ye all right in there?" Colin shouted through the massive oak door.

Brenna started at the sudden intrusion on her thoughts. "I'm fine Colin," she said as she clicked the send button. "I just needed a bit of time to collect my thoughts." She wasn't in the mood for company.

"I've brought yer supper."

"Just a second." She closed her laptop, then hobbled to the door. Opening it wide enough for him to enter, she forced a smile. Colin held a tray of something steaming, a full bottle of wine, and more importantly, an icepack. A peace offering of sorts. No doubt to buoy her spirits. Fat chance. At least she wouldn't have to traipse down to the kitchen.

The bottle of red was an Opus One. The man had taste; at one hundred and sixty dollars a bottle she wouldn't say no to a glass of that. She'd only had it twice before. Once at a fancy wine tasting fundraiser at the university, the other time with Jen to celebrate the day she earned her tenure at the university. Colin placed the tray on the writing desk.

“I’ll build ye a bit of a fire to take the chill out of the room.”

“Do you do all the cooking and cleaning around here? I thought there’d be staff to handle those trivialities,” Brenna said.

“I sent them on holiday when I learned ye were coming. Paid holiday. Including expenses.” He tossed a look at her over his shoulder. “They think I’ve lost my mind.”

“Yeah. I think the same thing, but for different reasons.” Brenna grabbed the steaming bowl of thick stew and dug in. “Not bad for a bachelor.”

Colin sat down next to her, relegating her pillow to the floor. “It’s all right. I’ll prepare ye to deal with Hafnar. We’ll begin in the morning.”

“How long do we have?”

“A couple of weeks at most.” He placed the icepack on her knee. “Ye’ll be just fine.”

Colin started the fire. He ensured it caught and was blazing before turning to leave her to her own thoughts. The bottle of Opus One called to her, and she debated whether to drink from the bottle or grab a glass. Propriety won and she grabbed both, along with a blanket, and sat in front of the fire.

She knew she would go. She had to. There was no chance of finding Lachlan’s family. She would have to look for him herself.

The first glass of wine, she savored. Full bodied richness with notes of new saddle leather, black fruits, roasted herbs, and burning embers powerful and rich with sweet tannin. She’d memorized the spiel given at the university fundraiser. Notes of new saddle leather? What the hell did that mean. By the third glass, she allowed herself to indulge in self-pity.

Embers glowed when she finally snapped out of her contemplative state, and the empty wine bottle stared ominously at her. A little unsteady, she wrapped herself in the blanket and laid her head down on the pillow of her arms, not bothering with the bed.

Sleep teased her, first inviting, then repulsing in fits and starts. Her subconscious pricked, reminding her she'd not checked in with Lachlan this evening. She called to him gently, a tenuous connection in her tipsy state.

Knee deep in water, through vacant eyes he noted her presence with a subtle shift of his weight. Standing taller, as if her company bolstered his courage. Time hung between them suspended from gossamer threads, their lives separated by the thinnest slice of magic.

A chill rippled down her legs, and she turned in the faux fur cocoon that hugged her, moving closer to the warm glow of dying embers. A sigh passed her lips, born of wanting him. A need rising within her, mirroring the tide that came for Lachlan, higher and higher until it would consume her.

Hazy thoughts bombarded her from too much wine. Thoughts of reaching beyond her vision and running her hand through Lachlan's raven hair. Fingers tracing the tendon that ran from jaw to shoulder. Her tongue tracing the path from his collarbone to his chest, stopping to lick the salt from his nipple. She wanted him.

The chill now gone, replaced with a tiny flicker of heat low in her belly. Imagining his touch raised the gooseflesh on her arms. She gasped and centered her attention on Lachlan, his eyes hooded, studying her.

He'd heard every thought.

She flung the blanket from her and slung one arm over her face to hide her embarrassment. "Too much wine, I'm sorry," she mumbled.

"Not nearly as sorry as I am, lass. I would give my soul to touch ye. For ye to touch me. I've felt nothing but frigid water and even colder stone at my back and beneath my feet. Salt that dries and itches and I cannot brush it away. Ye've changed my life, lass. This connection we share. What ye've allowed me to see through yer eyes has brought me more pleasure and peace than ye can imagine."

A flash of heat warmed her cheeks. "I. . .shouldn't have been thinking those things."

"I'm glad ye did. I thought perhaps it was only I that desired yer touch. It pleases me that ye desire mine as well. Find me, Brenna. Free me and let me touch ye the way ye imagined."

Brenna breathed deeply, closed her eyes, and tried to push aside the longing. It didn't budge. Instead, it snuggled right up next to her and spent the night.

CHAPTER NINE

A loud knock at her door startled her stomach into a back flip. “Yes?”

“Get a move on, Miss Sinclair. I’ll meet ye in the stable,” Colin said.

“It’s too dark. It can’t be morning yet.” She buried her head under the faux fur blanket and moaned, exhausted.

“It’s dark because it’s a fine Highland morning. The rain is coming down in sheets, and the sun will no show her face today. The stables, fifteen minutes.”

Crap.

She made it to the kitchen in five, wolfed down a muffin, then spent the next ten minutes washing it down with coffee. The man made a fine stew but couldn’t bake pastry to save his life.

True to his word, Colin awaited her outside Enbarr's stall. He sat on a large trunk, his back against the rails, his arms crossed in front of him. He looked a tad bit testy.

He rose from the footlocker and opened it. He removed a bundle of indigo velvet cloth, and a sword. The Answerer.

"That's what you call keeping them safe and sound? A trunk in a stable?" she said, her voice clipped.

"Sometimes the best hiding place is in plain sight," he said, tossing the sword from one hand to the other. "It's a broadsword with a two edged blade." He held it by the scabbard and handed it to her.

The moment she grasped the handle a surge of energy flowed up her arm and across her chest. She dropped it. It sent a plume of dust billowing up from the stable floor.

"What the hell was that?" she asked, backing away from the blade.

"Magic. It won't harm ye." He retrieved the sword and handed it to her a second time.

Another outpouring of magic rushed up her arm. This time, she held the handle tightly and pulled the protective leather away from the blade. It appeared untouched by time. The steel, highly polished, glinted in the dim light of the stable, and she detected an audible hum emanating from the blade. The hilt was intricately carved. Celtic knots wound their way from the base to the tip and the pommel held a brilliant faceted sapphire jewel.

Colin reached for the sword and secured the scabbard to it. "Best not to give Hafnar an open invitation," he said and returned it to her. "First lesson, grip. Yer grip on the handle must be fluid. Not too tight, nor too loose, so the sword can move in the hand. Align yer wrist with the hilt to get a correct grip. When ye strike a target, ye want the strength of yer arm behind it, not yer thumb. Ye must maintain a stance that allows good balance and ease of movement. Now, step out with yer right foot and keep yer feet shoulder width apart as much as possible. Never cross yer feet or bring them together as you move. Slide yer feet about an inch above the ground when you move so that if yer caught off guard you'll not be toppled over."

Brenna felt the subtle pressure of Lachlan pushing on the edges of her mind. She took the stance Colin directed and spoke to Lachlan.

"I'm in the middle of learning to fight with a sword."

"Excellent. I can help ye with that, lass. Yer right foot, step out with yer right foot." She did as he told her.

"It doesn't feel right." She put her left foot out front instead.

"The other right foot, Miss Sinclair," Colin said.

"It feels better if I lead with my left, why can't I just do it that way?"

"Because ye won't have proper leverage. Ye'll present a larger target to yer enemy, and ye won't have the reach. Yer chest will be forward of yer sword. Ye'll be run through before ye can blink. Try it again."

"He's right. Ye'll get used to how it feels."

"Now, to defend yerself against yer opponent's attacks, hold the sword in front of ye with the blade pointed up. Rotate yer arms and body to move the hilt of the sword to the left and right to defend against attacks to yer upper body and midsection." Brenna acted out his instructions. "Good, good. Now dip the point of the sword toward the ground to the appropriate side to defend against a blade headed for yer lower body."

"Block with the third of the sword closest to the hilt or ye'll be overpowered. Ye've not the strength yerself, so use the strength of the blade. Always choose to dodge rather than block if ye can. Ye'll have a better chance of counterattacking if yer sword is free."

"Focus, Miss Sinclair. Keep yer mind on the fight. If ye allow yer thoughts to drift, then no amount of training or skill can let ye win."

"Watch yer opponent. A subtle shift of weight or a glance will let ye know what he'll do next."

Colin reached inside the trunk, removed a blunted sword, and returned to stand in front of her. "Shall we dance, Miss Sinclair?" He grinned and wagged his eyebrows at her.

This was turning out to be entirely too much fun.

"Don't wait for him to make a move, lass. Right foot out, press forward, reach for his sword arm. Forward, forward, cut left to his knee."

The sword made contact. Hardly a nudge, but contact nonetheless.

"Good job, Miss Sinclair. Focus, I'm not dead yet and still in the fight. Don't be getting giddy just because ye tapped me."

She bit her lip to keep from smiling and pressed her opponent backwards.

"Right foot, Brenna. Right foot forward."

Too late. Colin's sword rapped her chest. Blunt tipped or not, it smarted. He swung his sword low and knocked her foot out from under her. Spinning in mid air, she landed hard on her ass, her back to Colin.

"Lay on yer back, now! Thrust the sword over yer head—aim for his bollocks."

She executed the move perfectly. Colin dropped his blade and fell to his knees. An anguished moan echoed in the stable, and he cupped his balls. "Bloody fucking hell."

Lachlan's laughter filled her head with its rich timbre, and she couldn't help but toss Colin's words back at him. "I'm not dead yet and still in the fight. Just because ye knocked me on my arse doesn't mean ye've bested me."

Colin lifted his face and slanted her a glare. She winked at him, and his grim look faltered until he finally laughed.

"Nicely done, Miss Sinclair." He rose to his feet, though it took a few seconds for him to stand straight.

"I think Lachlan and I have earned a gold star for the day, don't you?" She closed the gap between them and clapped him on the back. "Better luck next time, Colin."

"So that's yer secret. Ye had the help of a seasoned warrior. Brilliant idea. Ye fight well together. But we've only just started. En garde." Colin tapped her on the hip with the blunted sword and she stepped away bringing Answerer to bear on her foe.

"All right—another dance it is."

###

Five days of preparation, as Colin called it, left Brenna's muscles aching to the point she could barely walk or lift a fork. Every bit of her body protested, and still Colin insisted she continue honing her skills. She'd even covered herself with the cloak of invisibility and hidden in her room one afternoon to avoid another workout with the self-proclaimed drill sergeant.

She and Lachlan spent more and more time with their minds joined. He watched over her while she slept, coached her on the use of the sword, and told her she was brave to take on the task of finding and freeing him.

The sixth day dawned laden with iron clouds. A wall of fog rolled in, swallowing everything in its path.

"Must I practice today? I can't even lift my arms to wash my face, let alone lift that damn sword one more time. If the maker of the tapestry knew a woman was coming to help Lachlan, why isn't the sword lighter?" Brenna asked, picking at her breakfast.

"I assume that's a rhetorical question."

Brenna looked at him with a stone-faced stare.

"We've already discussed this, Miss Sinclair. The Sea God Manannan Mac Lir bestowed Clan MacGregor with Enbarr, who runs so swiftly that no adversary can catch him. A cloak woven with the powers of the Tuatha De Denaan that shields the wearer from all eyes, both fae and human so that they are invisible—"

"Yes, I know, and a great sword, the Answerer, which can cut through flesh like butter, creating wounds no healer could hope to cure."

"Right ye are, but the maker of the tapestry didn't devise how the relics would be used. Clan historians did. The sword weighs what it weighs and whining doesn't make it any lighter. Here," he said, shoving a bound book across the table. "Study this and we'll call it good. Lachlan will stay with ye today, eh?" he said, pushing his chair from the table. "I've a lead on Manannan Mac Lir's breastplate. It's the fourth item I'd like ye to take on the journey to find Lachlan. I'm going to check out the authenticity of the most recent rumor. I'll be gone two days. Three at the most. Stay put." He wagged a finger at her. "Study this book and practice with the sword. I'd say to stay off Enbarr and not tempt Hafnar, but ye'll only ride him anyway, so be careful. There are protective wards in place that encompass a hundred yard radius around the B&B. Ye should be fine while I'm away."

"Protective wards? What the heck does that mean?"

"A sorceress set spells along the perimeter of the property. Think of them as a magical keep out sign." He walked away without waiting for a response.

The book contained every scrap of knowledge Colin had about Faerie, Hafnar, Mannannan Mac Lir's gifts, the tapestry, the curse; everything he knew that might help her secure Lachlan's freedom.

"Well, I guess we know what we're doing today don't we?" she asked Lachlan.

"Aye, let's memorize the thing. Ought to be easy between the two of us. Perhaps the weather will blow over and we can fetch Enbarr for a ride."

"I was thinking exactly the same thing. As soon as Colin leaves." In the late afternoon, wicked May winds escorted the fog to oblivion, torturing the spring blooms surrounding the manor gatehouses, leaving them dead or dismembered. Horizontal rain pelted the windows beating out a staccato tune. They decided against a ride. Well, she did anyway. The thought of being unnecessarily wet and cold outweighed her desire to traipse across the countryside. Instead, they settled for watching Bridget Jones Diary and Brenna taught him the meaning of the term chick flick.

###

In the early evening, peals of laughter rang through the manor house. Lachlan was teaching Brenna how to play chess. They had quite a match going, but it was impossible to plan out her next move without Lachlan knowing what it would be. Naturally, she lost every game, but learned a few strategic moves along the way.

It was hours later, after BBC reruns of Sherlock, that Brenna realized Lachlan was gone. She couldn't put her finger on the moment he'd slipped away. High tide no doubt, and yet, desolation oozed through her veins like a slow poison invading her body.

"Lachlan?" she said, reaching for him.

Nothing. Not even the flicker of a connection.

Brenna waited half an hour and tried again.

And again.

Panic punched her in the gut. She watched the second hand on her watch tick through time and counted each movement for sixty long minutes, all the while, desperately seeking a link to Lachlan.

Something was horribly wrong.

At last, a whisper-thin bond formed. He stood in thigh high water. She'd never seen him look as forlorn as he did in that moment. His face, drawn and haggard, his eyes dull and clouded when he gazed at her, aware at last of her presence.

"Something is amiss, lass. I'm getting weaker. I feel as though. . .I'm running out of time."

Brenna's heart didn't quite stop. It hesitated for long moments then beat like a jackhammer within the confines of her chest. *It's the curse.* "I'm coming, I'm leaving this very minute."

Keep calm and carry on, please, don't die.

Minutes later, Brenna had her saddlebag packed and slung over her shoulder. As she made her way to the stable, storm clouds hovered on the horizon, roiling silver gray against the blackness of the night.

Enbarr paced in his stall, alert and in tune with Brenna's mood. Approaching his pen with trepidation, she closed her eyes and reached out with her mind to soothe the stallion. He came to her and snorted moist hot breath onto her face, surprising her. She blinked open her eyes and held his gaze, then made quick work of saddling him. She sensed Enbarr knew the time had come to serve his master. She retrieved Manannan Mac Lir's relics from the footlocker and secured them to Enbarr's saddle.

Brenna mounted, her nerves strung tight in anticipation. Enbarr bolted from the stable. They traveled stealthily by the sliver of moonlight, maneuvering over the terrain.

CHAPTER TEN

Answerer hung securely on Enbarr's left side for a right-handed draw from the scabbard. She ran her hand lightly down the worn leather sheath holding the powerful blade. Her arm tingled with its magic. It hummed in anticipation of the moment she would release it and it would free Lachlan.

Magic. Faeries. Immortal men, women, and beasts. A sorceress, even. She was glad her mind opened to the possibility of the impossible.

They traveled for twenty long hours with only pit stops to relieve Brenna's bladder. Enbarr spared her his preternatural speed and alternated between a canter and a gallop. When her body could no longer take the pounding, she drew back on the reins. She slipped gracefully from the saddle into a heap on the ground. Her legs, numb and weak, refused to hold her weight.

She reclined on the terrain, closed her eyes, and waited for the blood to return to her legs.

The worst of the waves of tingles traveling to her toes ceased, and she sat upright. With a deep breath, she hauled herself up off the field. Food. A can of soup would help restore her strength. *Hot* soup would be even better, but she lacked the energy to build a fire. She fumbled in the saddlebags and pulled out a can of clam chowder. Next, she dug for the P-38 in her pants pocket. The tiny folding can opener was the Army's greatest little invention.

Two bites into her one course meal, and Lachlan nudged at the edge of her awareness.

"Oh, thank God." Brenna's hands trembled. "I was afraid…that I'd lost you."

Lachlan shook his head. "I don't understand what's happening. Why do I grow weaker?"

She had no choice now, but to tell him. She revealed what she knew of the curse Hafnar had spelled him with.

Lachlan mustered the strength to stand tall and proud despite his bindings. "So help me, Danu, I will kill him with my bare hands." It was not an idle threat. "I will not die before I see ye in the flesh before me. I *will* live long enough to touch ye, Brenna. I *will* hold ye in my arms. He will not take that from me. I swear it."

Hafnar was a dead man. Revenge was a powerful motivator, and as long as it fueled Lachaln's physical stamina, she didn't care one iota. She'd broach the subject of Hafnar's rehabilitation later. Much later. When Lachlan was a free man. Fear snuck up on her and niggled at her. What if she failed to find him in time? Her skin crawled at the thought, and she shivered.

"You know what I'm thinking, don't you?" Brenna said.

“Aye, don’t fret, lass. Death is a welcome reprieve from how I’ve existed these last centuries. Were I to die now, I would be grateful. My only regret would be what we might have shared together.”

“A few hours of rest, and I’ll be back on the trail. I just need a couple of hours.”

Brenna blew out the breath she’d been holding, ruffling her bangs. A flash of light caught her attention. Hundreds of fireflies clustered around her in a cloud of twinkling light. With a spoonful of soup half way to her mouth, she froze, her mouth agape in wonder.

They weren’t fireflies at all. One tiny creature settled on the edge of her spoon, cocked it’s head, and stared at her.

“Do you see what I see?” Brenna asked.

Lachlan smiled, but said nothing.

Another hovered directly in front of her, its tiny wings fluttering like those of a hummingbird. They disbursed and scattered in all directions. They returned with bits of leaves and twigs and then hundreds of them gathered with a log, and then two. They whizzed and whirled, darting back and forth, until a flame flickered in the makeshift campfire they’d set upon making for her. Then, they disbursed on a breeze and were gone.

“Sprites, lass. It’s rare they show themselves.”

“My gosh, why would they build me a fire?”

“You are with Enbarr. They know he is Fae. It’s unconscionable he would be with a human unless there was great trust and loyalty between ye. It was out of respect they showed themselves and granted ye the gift of fire.”

She shook her head in disbelief and wondered if long hours in the saddle had rattled her brain.

Nope.

The fire was real and warm. "Wow. That was incredible. I'm not delirious, am I? Or hallucinating?"

Lachlan chuckled. "Nay, lass. Ye didn't imagine them."

The list of faerie tale creatures come to life grew again. She could now add Sprites to the tally. She grabbed the wool blanket stowed behind Enbarr's saddle and wrapped it around herself. She used her spoon and a stick to place her can of soup near the flames to warm it a bit. A full belly and a few hours' sleep and then she'd be off.

The clam chowder sated her hunger. She lay down and dozed until the fire died down to embers. The chilled air woke her. She gathered her few belongings and doused the fire with handfuls of dirt.

"Mount," she thought. Enbarr obeyed and she threw a leg over the beast. He rose up on all fours and galloped ever closer to Lachlan.

###

Two days. Two frustrating days of failing to locate Lachlan. Hard ground and cold food in the wilds of the Highlands. Enbarr saw no reason to stick to the roads, or pass a motel, or even take a well-worn path. To him the only route was a straight line to his intended target and it was most certainly, the road less traveled. But she didn't mind. Not really, anyway. Any suffering she might face on her quest was nothing compared to the centuries Lachlan had endured. Even Hafnar's stunts paled by comparison.

The days, thankfully, were curiously absent of rain, and though the wind had picked up now that they rode closer to the shoreline, the temperature was pleasant enough. Brisk and invigorating, it kept her mind sharp and alert. At last, they reached the westernmost shore of

Scotland. From there they continued north along the coast.

Late in the afternoon of the second day, they crested a rise and descended into a village. It was a tiny community, whose survival depended on the ocean and its bounty.

Enbarr led her through the town, over the brow of a hill and down to the sandy expanse of shore. He walked headlong into the ocean before Brenna took charge of the reins.

In the distance, an island rose from the depths of sapphire like a shrine to an ancient Celtic god. Waves broke against the craggy cliffs, and a waterfall gushed over the top in hara-kiri against the rocky shore hundreds of feet below.

She dismounted and pulled out the handheld GPS unit Colin had equipped her with and fiddled with the various settings until it spit out the name of the island in the distance. Skye.

"Okay, Enbarr. The Isle of Skye it is. I don't doubt your ability to swim my friend, but I think I'll find us a ferry." Brenna turned the beast around and headed into town to arrange passage to Skye.

Odd looks from the inhabitants of the small fishing village were tossed her way. They had progressed enough into the twenty first century that walking the ocean side of the street with a horse in tow was peculiar.

She reached for Lachlan. It took a few moments, but he gathered enough strength to stay connected with her for a few hours at a time in the last day. He was still exhausted, but seemed to have been granted a reprieve.

"I think we're close now, Lachlan. There is an island off the coast of Scotland that Enbarr seems intent on taking me to. There's not much beyond it but the sea. I can only assume you are somewhere on that isle."

He nodded and flashed her a halfhearted smile, then dropped his chin to his chest.

At the farthest end of town, a two story pink building caught her eye. A wooden sign in the postage stamp front yard indicated there was a room available for the night.

Brenna crossed the street, tied Enbarr to the white picket fence, and entered the inn. The man behind the counter was young, tall, and skinny with shocking red hair and a splash of freckles across his cheekbones.

"Well, hello, lovely lady. What can I do for you?" he said, without even a hint of an accent.

"I need a room for the night and. . .maybe a spot in the back yard for my horse." She smiled sheepishly.

"Horse? Well that is an odd request. You arrived on horseback?" He rapped his fingers on the counter, thinking. "We don't exactly have a hitching post out back, but you're welcome to figure something out. There'll be an extra fee, of course." He winked at her.

"Of course." Brenna winked back. She had the feeling the extra fee would find its way directly into his wallet.

"The dining room opens at five; you can order room service if you like. It'll just be the one night?"

"Yes. The ferry to Skye, what time is the first run tomorrow?" Brenna asked.

"Brriiigghht and early at six."

"Perfect. I'll be on it." Brenna pulled out a wad of Colin's cash from the front pocket of her jeans and prepaid the bill. After taking Enbarr to the back of the building, unsaddling him, and conveying to him to stick close by, she headed for her room on the second floor.

The room was small and feminine with flowered curtains, a matching comforter, and rose colored carpeting. Rather quaint really, but too girlie for her taste. Brenna threw herself across the mattress and groaned with pleasure. Sleeping in the open on hard earth made the lumpy mattress feel like a feather bed at a five star hotel. Not that Brenna had actually ever stayed in a five star hotel, but she could imagine. It was a relief not to have to sleep on the cold ground with pebbles that poked.

Brenna kicked off her shoes. "I'm taking a nice long scalding hot bath," she said to Lachlan.

The bathroom was a throwback to another time. A time when pink tile was in vogue. The claw footed tub was overlarge for the closet sized room and was angled slightly in order to fit into its allotted space.

"If you're staying, close your eyes." She peeled off her clothing and turned on the hot water full blast. The pipes rattled and shook as the tub filled, and she hoped nothing would burst.

"Are ye sure I can't just sneak a peek?" Lachlan asked. "I could be dead any moment."

She sank into the porcelain envelope. Her hair floated in the water around her like jellyfish tentacles undulating softly in a tide pool. "That is *not* funny."

Apparently, Lachlan thought humor made his situation seem less dire.

Tendrils of hair tickled her cheek, floated under her chin and submerged to rest tranquilly across her neck. She closed her eyes and focused on her breathing, inhaling deeply and sending the breath to the parts of her body that pained her, letting the breath swirl about the ache and wash it from her body with each exhalation.

"Lass."

"Mmmm."

"Yer the most beautiful woman I've ever laid my eyes on." His voice was so soft, she could barely hear his whisper.

Her eyes flew open and she gasped. He pinned her in place with nothing more than his hooded gaze. "You're peeking."

"I am. And if I'm not mistaken, ye don't really mind."

It wasn't a question, but a statement. And he was right. So very, very right.

She sank lower in the tub, but she knew the water didn't obstruct his view. Annoyed with her hair swirling around her, she grabbed a handful, intent on twisting it into a bun to cushion her head against the hard surface of the tub. The strands wrapped insistently around her throat like tentacles and annoyance gave way to horror. She struggled to lift her head from the water and failed. Her head slammed against the tub. Stars exploded before her eyes like fireworks and blinded her. She shrieked in horror and managed a breath before her head was thrust below the water, held there by invisible hands, determined to choke the life from her.

She struggled to loosen the grasp around her neck by kicking and thrashing, turning and twisting. Nothing worked. The hair, so tightly strung around her neck, sliced into her flesh. Her vision clouded with the red haze of her blood swirling with the bath water.

Lachlan bellowed, "Hafnar, you fucking bastard. Leave her be!"

Hafnar roared with laughter. "Just having a bit of fun, brother."

Brenna used her toes to yank the chain attached to the plug keeping the tub from draining. Instead of clawing at the hair cutting her neck, she used her hands to splash water out of the tub. At last she could breathe.

She glimpsed Hafnar and watched as Lachlan struggled against his manacles. The muscles in his neck strained and blood oozed from his wrists. "Enough." His voice reverberated throughout the cavern, echoing.

Hafnar disappeared and the insane laughter ceased.

Brenna folded herself into a fetal position and sobbed.

"It's all right, lass. He's gone."

Brenna wept harder.

"Look at me." His voice rang loud and clear.

Brenna fought to collect her rampant emotions and lifted her face. The waterworks continued but slowed as she took deep, slow breaths.

"Yer all right. Do ye hear me? Yer all right. He was toying with us. It's a game to him. He cannot kill you, remember?"

She pulled the hair away from her neck and felt along the cut with her fingers. The oozing had slowed and would stop in no time. She nodded in agreement. All modesty gone, she crawled out of the tub and wrapped herself in a towel.

"Soon, my Brenna. Soon, I will be with ye and I'll keep ye from harm. I promise."

CHAPTER ELEVEN

The crossing to the Isle of Skye was uneventful, and they arrived at its shore just as the sun turned the sky a brilliant shade of coral and chased away the murky grey of first light. Enbarr led Brenna in a northeasterly direction along the sheer cliffs of Skye.

"Hafnar's been strangely quiet since I left the B&B. Do you think he'll be waiting for us?" Brenna asked Lachlan.

"Yes. I've little doubt he'll try to hamper us one last time. As to his absence of late, he's prone to dramatics. I can only guess he's planning something particularly dreadful for us."

Lachlan was bone-weary. His fading immortality and the effort to stay connected to her was taking its toll on him. "It's almost over, Lachlan. Just hold on awhile longer, okay?"

He nodded and she let the connection fade so he could conserve his strength.

Several hours passed in solitude. Enbarr slowed his pace and finally halted in his tracks, sampling the air with his ebony snout. He seemed unsure for a moment, then shook his head, black mane rippling, and drew closer to the cliff. Brenna tensed as they neared the precipice, remembering the barreling wind Hafnar had conjured to throw her down the side of the cliff at Lachlan's castle. Her breathing grew shallow and adrenaline started pumping, preparing her to face her enemy. She listened intently for the wind to howl, but heard nothing except the crashing waves below.

Enbarr continued along the edge of the cliff for several hundred yards before finding the narrow craggy path that lead in a switchback pattern down the side of the escarpment. Narrow being the operative word.

The thought of traveling up the side of the rock face on the return trip had Brenna scanning the area for an alternate route.

Anxiety rose with every step. The air, heavy with salt and tension, weighed her down. Stones skittered over the edge in a race to the bottom, and she gasped as Enbarr stumbled. Brenna's heart beat wildly as they trekked downward toward their destination. Enbarr stopped on the path and lifted his head, listening.

Precious silent moments ticked away on an invisible clock while Enbarr stood, waiting, listening for something. The sound started so quietly she almost missed it.

Brenna looked down at the path, and the smallest of the pebbles that lined it vibrated and skittered.

"Shit." She gently squeezed her thighs against Enbarr's flanks and urged him forward. She extended her thoughts to him in reassurance.

She leaned lower across his back, helping to guide him down the trail as his second pair of eyes. His muscles quivered with restrained power as they descended toward the shore.

The rumbling and tumbling of stones over the edge of the sheer cliff intensified and she loosened one hand from the white knuckled grip on the reins and ran it over her scar, blood pressure ticking up a degree.

Keep calm and carry on. Keep calm and carry on.

Faster, Enbarr. You must move faster.

Terrified, she dug her heels into Enbarr's flanks and gave him no choice but to obey. A scream formed in her chest. She gritted her teeth and swallowed hard to keep it contained.

Faster, Enbarr, please.

Finally, they reached the solid sliver of shoreline and galloped in an easterly direction along the edge of the cliff they had just descended. A shock wave of sound thundered and Brenna looked back. A rock slide obliterated the path they'd descended. "Screw you, Hafnar! You missed me!"

She was safe. For now.

Another few hundred yards down shore and Enbarr stopped. Brenna squeezed his flanks with her thighs, urging him to continue, but he nickered and threw his head back in annoyance, stomping his foot.

She dismounted and inspected the cliff face. Her gaze journeyed up and down the rock face looking for the reason for Enbarr's refusal to budge. Her visual inspection revealed nothing.

Enbarr stomped his foot again, clearly agitated.

She felt along the surface of the stone and her hand disappeared into thin air.

Magic.

This was it. This is what they'd searched for. Lachlan was so close now she shivered.

"That's it, the mouth of the cavern is right there," she said, unable to keep her voice from raising an octave. "The tide is coming in, Enbarr. We probably have an hour at best."

Brenna urged the beast through the opening of the cave and dismounted. Where the hell was Hafnar, now?

Stay here my friend.

Brenna removed the Answerer from Enbarr's saddle and slung it over her shoulder, then grabbed a flashlight from the saddlebag and tucked it under her arm. She tossed the cloak of invisibility over her shoulders and shimmered out of sight.

Inky darkness shrouded her within twenty feet of the cave entrance and she clicked on the light. The stone floor had worn smooth over the centuries, but a few large rocks impinged on the path and slowed her progress.

Another hundred yards and the narrow cavern passageway opened into a voluminous cave that arched high above her. Torches, lit with magic, hung from wrought iron holders and ringed the circumference of the den casting a golden glow.

She didn't move. Or make a sound. Or breathe.

Brenna clutched the cloak, hid the flashlight in its folds, and pulled it taut around her. Her jaw dropped and her mind spun at the sight before her.

Turquoise and silver scales covered the beast and shimmered like a pool of water in the torchlight. A horny crest formed on the top of its serpentine head and ran the length of its back to the tip of a spear shaped tail.

One eye opened, silver with a reptilian slit pupil. The other eye remained closed as if the beast were deciding whether the intrusion was worth getting up for. It opened its mouth and yawned, revealing needle sharp teeth. Wide nostrils flared as it took in her scent.

A dragon.

Instinct burst through her momentary paralysis, and invisibly cloaked, she ran to the left of the cave, making her way to the passageway that continued into the cavern directly behind the dragon sentry. She knew she had to get to that passageway in order to reach Lachlan. She sensed his presence and reached for him. Their connection flickered, but didn't take.

Forgetting herself, she yelled, "Lachlan, I'm here." The dragon screeched and she ran faster.

Brenna disappeared down the passageway behind the dragon's back. Fueled by fear, she ran. She would not stop, could not stop, and one foot pounded in front of the other. She cast a glance over her shoulder. The dragon was much too large to follow her. She refused to think ahead to when she and Lachlan would have to cross its path again.

Keep calm and carry on. . .keep calm and carry on.

The cloak caught between her legs and sent her splaying onto the cavern floor. The flashlight flew out of her grasp and landed in a puddle. Her newly healed knee ripped open and a surge of pain flooded her. She scrambled to her feet, abandoned the cloak, retrieved the flashlight, and hobbled through the tunnel. Adrenaline kicked in and numbed the pain. She hobbled faster and her eyes followed the beam of light through the darkness.

The echo of the sea pricked her ears and urged her forward. The tunnel curved sharply ahead. She rounded the corner and halted. He'd heard her approach. His verdant eyes weakened her knees and turned her bones to pudding. He was taller than she expected. And broader. Her heart pummeled her chest and her lungs burned from forgetting to exhale. "Lachlan."

He pinned her with a look. "My Brenna, yer here. At last, yer here."

Brenna drew the Answerer from its scabbard and closed the distance between them. "Pull the chains taut, Lachlan," she said, and raised the sword above her head to impart the freeing blows, "Don't move. Whatever you do, don't move."

She swung the blade and Answerer cleaved cleanly through the chain. Another blow from the great sword and a second chain fell away.

Lachlan's arms fell freely to his side for the first time in six hundred years.

Onto his knees he fell, and Brenna heaved the sword twice more to free his ankles. She knelt beside him and he enfolded her in his arms. A glacial chill penetrated her clothing, his body biting cold. He pulled away and held her face in his hands, his eyes locked on hers.

He slanted his mouth over hers and flames erupted and zinged through her veins. His tongue invaded her senses and the coiled knot in her belly grew impossibly tighter. "I can never repay ye, lass, but I'll give ye my heart if ye'll have it," he said, a husky edge to his voice.

She nodded, dumbfounded by his declaration. A section of chain dangled from each manacle. "Hold still while I get the manacles." Brenna fumbled with the sword. Her hands shook as she slipped the blade beneath the final bit of the metal at Lachlan's wrists and ankles and sliced through the last of the faerie magic that bound him. The manacles fell away and clattered on the stone floor of the cavern.

"We have to hurry. The tide is coming in and there's a dragon in there," she said, casting her head over her shoulder in the direction of the beast.

"Breathe, lass. Ye've done yer part. It's my turn now." He rose from his knees, bringing Brenna up with him.

A blaze of heat rippled from her breast and spread across her cheeks in a flash of fire. Strong arms engulfed her in an embrace and try though she might to maintain control her emotions, the tears streamed down her face. He swept them away with a gentle caress of his hands. When he lowered his face and touched his lips to hers, her knees buckled. He slipped an arm behind her legs and cradled her in his arms.

"You've hurt yerself," he said, noticing the blood from her wound.

"It'll be fine, but put me down, you'll need your strength to face—"

"Don't fret, lass. Hafnar's spell stole my powers, but you've released me. The power of Fae flows freely in my veins now, not hampered by Hafnar's chains. I'll be right as rain in no time." He flexed his arms. A ruddy hue colored to his cheeks and the gaunt haggardness disappeared from his eyes.

She had done it then. She'd halted the curse. Relief swept through her and she shivered.

Lachlan stepped toward the corridor.

"The sword," Brenna said.

"Aye. We'll likely need that." Lachlan knelt down and she retrieved the instrument of his freedom.

He refused to let her go and began to make his way toward the only obstacle that stood between them and freedom.

The dragon.

Lachlan spared a moment to retrieve the cloak of invisibility. His gait grew stronger and more purposeful with each step he took toward his enemy.

They reached the end of the first passageway, and Lachlan placed Brenna on her feet. "I want ye to be safe, lass, so you'll keep the cloak and stay to the edge of the cave. Keep moving toward the other passage as quickly as ye can. Don't stop, and don't look back, do ye understand me, lass? Use the sword if ye must."

"I'll keep the cloak, but you take the sword. If it attacks, you'll need it to defend yourself." She handed him the blade.

Lachlan took her hand and pulled her into the lighted cavern to meet their foe. He pushed her rather unceremoniously to one side of the cave and ran in the opposite direction. "Hurry, lass. My fighting skills are a bit rusty."

The tremendous scaled snout lifted. Its nostrils flared, scenting Lachlan. The great turquoise iridescent head swung in his direction. Silver eyes grew wide, and its horned crest rose in warning. Its lips curled away from serrated teeth, and without a visible inhale of breath, it blew a ribbon of fire at Lachlan.

He ducked and tucked, then rolled to avoid the flame. The air filled with the sound of indignant cursing.

Lachlan stepped closer to the dragon and held the Answerer toward his enemy. The beast reared back on its hind legs and spread its leathery wings. It opened its maw. The beast filled its lungs with air and hesitated. It held the breath. Catching her scent, the dragon turned and looked in Brenna's direction, but the cloak kept her hidden. The mythical monster returned his attention to the immediate threat of Lachlan, shifting its bulk onto its hind legs.

Brenna continued to edge along the cavern wall, eyes on the beast, hands sliding along the wall of the cave as a guide to keep her moving in the direction she sought. The dragon took a breath and searched for her again.

Her knee screamed with each step, and silver eyes followed her scent. He smelled her blood she was sure of it. The screech of metal on stone pained her ears. She noticed then for the first time, the chains and manacles that held the beast to the cavern floor. A prisoner, just as Lachlan had been.

Lachlan took advantage of the dragon's hesitation and swung Answerer furiously towards his mark.

"Stop!" The word echoed in the cavern. "He's chained."

Too late. A shriek of pain reverberated in the cave and blood spewed from the gash inflicted across the dragon's chest. Lachlan's eyes fell to the manacles, and he halted his attack.

The beast swung its great head in her direction confused by the sound emanating out of seemingly nowhere. Brenna dropped the hood of the cloak and the dragon stretched its neck until his snout was within inches of her face.

The silver eyes held no fear. No malice. They held something altogether unexpected.

Sorrow.

Pain.

Desperation.

Brenna reached out with her mind. Images assailed her rather than thoughts. Memories perhaps, of a burning village, people screaming in horror as flames burned them alive.

"You killed all those people?" Brenna stepped back and flattened herself against the cavern wall, shocked by the carnage she had seen.

The monster swung its serpent head from side to side and one last image pressed at the edges of Brenna's mind.

Hafnar. High in the sky above the ruined village upon the back of his black dragon.

The beast before her, a victim of Hafnar's evil, had no more desire to carry out its mission of keeping Lachlan prisoner than Lachlan wanted to be at the end of the passageway waiting to drown at every high tide.

"Free him," she said, and she looked directly into the eyes of the beast.

The dragon lowered its head to the floor of the cave, as if paying homage to her. She knew without a doubt that the dragon understood her words.

Lachlan hesitated to carry out Brenna's request. "What if yer wrong, lass?"

"I'm not."

Lachlan hesitated for only a moment before he swung the Answerer in a tight circle above his head and lunged forward for the blow that would free one leg from its bondage. The dragon didn't flinch. It moved its position slightly to allow Lachlan access to the chains that bound the other leg. The second swing, as precise as the first, freed the beast.

"I don't know how you'll get out of here. You're too large to fit through the passageway, but at least you can move a bit now," Lachlan said.

The dragon bowed before Lachlan respectfully.

"Wait, we can't leave him here. There must be a way to get him out," Brenna said.

"Lass, we must hurry," Lachlan said.

The dragon moaned, and Brenna felt him push at her mind. A single word resonated from his thoughts. *"Go."*

"We'll come back for you, dragon, I swear it." She reached a hand out and the dragon nuzzled her palm. "I swear it."

They turned away from the beast, unable to help him beyond what they had already done, at least for the moment, and continued down the path to the shore.

The little bit of daylight that pierced the entrance, pooled and reflected on the surface of the tide that toyed with their ankles. Lachlan's gaze rested on the ripples of light at his feet.

Daylight. He seemed to marvel at his first glimpse of it. He stopped and looked at his fingers lit in the sun and examined his shadow.

Enbarr nickered in recognition of his master and stomped his feet impatiently. Lachlan stepped forward and embraced the beast around his neck. He stroked the length of Enbarr's shoulder.

Lachlan took the reins and reached for Brenna's hand and they stepped into the sunlight beyond the cave. Ten steps down the shore and Lachlan clenched her hand and he maneuvered her behind him. Hafnar waited for them. Hands on hips, he grinned.

"Free at last, free at last, eh, brother?" Long blond hair lifted on the ocean breeze and whisky colored eyes glittered with malice. "Enjoy it for the next few minutes. Before I snatch it from you once more." The smile disappeared and he looked beyond where they stood. His gaze fixed on something behind them.

Brenna turned, afraid to take her eyes off Hafnar for even the single second it took to evaluate what was happening in the background.

The man who stood at the mouth of the cavern was taller than Lachlan, easily six foot six or seven. His hair was black as jet, almost blue. Blood oozed from the open slash at his chest.

His eyes.

His eyes glowed silver.

CHAPTER TWELVE

Brenna's eyes grew wide as she realized the dragon and the stranger were one. She closed her eyes against the sun and shook her head. She drew a deep breath and peeked beneath her lashes. He was real all right.

Hafnar glared at the stranger. "I see your new friends freed you as well. You had a duty to me. I had your word you'd guard the bastard."

"My word wasn't given freely. Ye ripped it from me when you killed the villagers in my little piece of the world and threatened the lives of the ones I love," the man said.

"You and your family were nothing. I had every right to use your skills to my advantage," Hafnar said, arrogance rolling off him.

The stranger stepped forward and together, the men marched toward Hafnar, and he deeper into the swirling waters of the sea. A highland battle cry rent the air as both men charged, The Answerer raised for battle. Lachlan swung for Hafnar's neck, the stranger, weaponless, lunged for his knees. Neither landed a blow as Hafnar shifted into thin air, reappearing twenty feet down shore.

"Bloody hell," Lachlan bellowed at the failed attempt. Sweat beaded at his temple and his chest heaved with effort. His movements were stiff, his body unused to its new found freedom.

"Get yerselves to safety. I'll hold him off the best I can," the stranger said to Lachlan. "Your woman is injured."

"No. We stand together," Lachlan said.

Lachlan pushed at the edge of Brenna's mind. "*Take Enbarr and get to safety. Hurry, lass.*"

A high-pitched whistle erupted from between Lachlan's teeth. The horse responded immediately. Enbarr knelt before her, and she threw a leg over his broad back. She grabbed hold of the reins and Enbarr ran full tilt down the shoreline.

Up ahead the cliffs tapered down toward the sea. Enbarr headed for the place where the cliff barely rose above the shore. They raced across the rising tide.

The frigid water that Enbarr kicked up as he ran dissipated the adrenaline crashing through Brenna's veins. Her lungs constricted, and her eyes blurred with unshed tears. She fought against the mini meltdown that threatened.

Enbarr leapt from the shore to the cliff. A few steps upward, and they were on dry ground. She reined him in and turned to view the scene they'd left behind.

Brenna didn't know what she expected to see, but it was not what unfolded several hundred yards down shore. Hafnar, down on one knee, apparently begging for mercy at the feet of a turquoise and silver dragon. Lachlan swung Answerer in a tight arc and unleashed the power in the blade. The sword bit deeply into Hafnar's ribs and a river of crimson flowed into the sea.

"Oh my God," were the only words that tumbled from her mouth.

Outnumbered, injured, and apparently out of magic, Hafnar faded into a shadow of grey. The obscure haze swirled and vanished like smoke in the wind.

The waves crashed the shore. Fast and furious the tide climbed. Enbarr pranced anxiously seeming to want to return for Lachlan. The stallion quieted when Lachlan threw a leg up and over the back of the dragon. Brenna was rendered speechless. The dragon circled and touched down with the grace of a butterfly. Lachlan dismounted, and long strides ate up the ground that separated him from Brenna. He pulled her off Enbarr to cradle her in his arms. He held her tight, and she burst into an all-out crying fit. She hid her face against his chest.

Kneeling on the ground with her still in his arms, he rocked her back and forth, whispering Gaelic endearments in her ear.

"Why all the tears?" Lachlan asked.

"I can't help myself. I'm just so relieved that I won't have to watch you drown again, that I. . .I can't believe we found you. That you're here. . .and alive. . .and free."

He pulled away from her, tilted her face back, and lost himself in her steel grey eyes.

"Let's go home, please," Brenna said.

Rising from the ground, he set Brenna down on her own two feet. "Hafnar has gone. I doubt forever, but we can hope for a few hours of peace while he licks his wounds. Let's be on our way."

Lachlan turned his attention to his prison mate. The air shimmered like a heat wave rising off asphalt in the summer. The dragon disappeared, and in its stead appeared the man who had emerged from the cavern.

The man dragon dropped to one knee and bowed his head.

"My name is Soren. I owe yer lady a debt I will repay with my life if I must. She freed me when others would have annihilated me. I mean no harm to ye nor her and swear an oath my debt shall be repaid." Soren's voice rang with conviction.

"Come with us then. If Hafnar thinks to surprise us again, we'll stand together," Lachlan said. He lifted Brenna onto Enbarr and settled himself behind her. A winged shadow fell over them as Soren lifted to the air.

###

Lachlan's heart drummed in his chest. He was a free man, at last.

Wanting nothing more than to give Enbarr his head and use whatever speed he could get from the Fae horse, he hesitated. It was more important that Brenna have a chance to rest. That, and he didn't trust himself in the saddle just yet. It'd been awhile.

The longing to be home was outweighed only by his desire to hold onto the woman who sat astride his horse in front of him. He hadn't expected his heart to leap from his chest or his blood to pool in his loins when he saw her in the flesh for the first time. He wanted nothing more than to protect her and keep her safe. She had risked much by coming for him, and he was grateful.

But if he was honest with himself, he wanted more from her. Desire for her caused a painful swelling between his thighs. Her luscious backside pounding into his front side with Enbarr's every stride did nothing to dispel a hunger left unsated for centuries.

He brushed the hair away from her long, slender neck and placed a kiss on the tender spot behind her ear. She inhaled at the touch of his lips and held her breath for long moments before leaning back against his chest and expelling the air from her lungs.

Warmth flooded him. She was so toasty warm. He tightened his grip, pulled her closer, and let her heat saturate his long frozen bones.

By late afternoon, Enbarr had transported them to the edge of Skye where a ferryboat waited to return them to the shores of Scotland. Enbarr pranced on board and Lachlan dismounted, helping Brenna descend to her feet. They got underway immediately. White caps spit salted water, soaking them. Soggy clothes gave Brenna a case of the shakes. She slid down onto the damp deck, tucked up her leg to her chest and rested her forehead on her one good knee.

Lachlan removed her boot and rolled up her pant leg to inspect her injury. Brenna flinched when a tug removed the material from the clotted wound, causing fresh blood to ooze. It was swollen, angry red, and hot to the touch.

A deck hand ran to do Lachlan's bidding and returned with a first aid kit to tend the laceration.

Lachlan leaned closer to Brenna and whispered, "I was expecting whisky and strips of cloth to bind the wound. I've no idea what to do with this box."

Brenna beamed at him, and her smile knocked the breath from his lungs. She took the kit from him and flipped open the plastic latches. She rifled around and came up with hand sanitizer. She squeezed a glob into her palm and motioned for Lachlan to do the same. "This will kill the germs that are on our hands and could get into the wound and cause problems."

"Germs?"

She fumbled some more with the pack, setting aside antiseptic cleansing wipes a roll of gauze and first aid tape. "Tiny microscopic. . .never mind. It will clean your hands."

Lachlan took the items from her. "Which one first?" he asked.

"The antiseptic cleansing wipes. That will kill any germs in the wound."

"Hrmph. More germs."

Lachlan opened the package and wiped away the dirt and grime from her knee. His hands lingered on her bare calf caressing the ivory skin as he disinfected the wound. Smooth as silk and shapely with lean muscle. His gaze continued to her delicate foot.

"What the bloody hell is this?" he asked, inspecting her big toe.

"It's toenail polish. Matches my fingernails, see?"

The hopeful tone of her voice and the hint of a glint in her eyes told Lachlan she hoped he was pleased.

Indeed he was, particularly with the buttercream feel of her leg. "The world is a very different place than when I left it."

"I'll explain it all to you. You'll be up to speed in no time." Her enthusiasm was palpable and her words reassured him, though he had his doubts.

He wrapped the gauze around her knee and secured it with tape. She shivered from being wet and cold and Lachlan sat beside her, wrapping her in his arms.

Once they arrived at the port of the small fishing village and disembarked, Lachlan handed Brenna up into the saddle and led Enbarr by the reins. Lachlan stopped once they crested the rise separating the shore from the town. The tiny village bustled in the late afternoon of the spring day.

At ease with a sword and trained in the art of war, he didn't expect a shiver of unrest to ripple his long unused muscles. His heart beat harder and faster as he saw for the first time how completely his world had changed.

Brenna had called them cars. They were everywhere, some moving some not. Tall, round wooden sentinels spaced a hundred paces apart sprouted from the land. Trees with no branches, one attached to the other with thick strands of. . .something. He knew not their purpose. Some strands crossed the blackened carriage paths and held rectangles of red, green, and yellow light. Their purpose seemed to signal commands to the cars. All of the women he could see were wearing trews. He'd seen Brenna wear them, but thought it an anomaly; not so.

"I should like to eat, lass. Where can we find food here?" He didn't require food or drink or sustenance of any kind. But he'd been craving a good, thick steak for the last two hundred years.

"This way," she said and pointed in the direction they needed to go. "The inn where I stayed last night. We can eat, get a room, and you can take a nice hot shower."

"Shower?" He cocked an eyebrow.

Brenna flashed him one of her radiant smiles. "You've seen one. It's a tall walled box that rains inside. You're going to love it, I promise.

People stared as they passed by. Some even looked terrified. A powerful warhorse carrying a bloodied lass led by a warrior with a sword strapped across his back, looking every bit the barbarian.

"We've several hours of daylight left. Enbarr can cover a vast stretch in that time. Perhaps we should continue on. We'll find a place to sleep under the stars," he said.

"Oh no. I am not spending another night roughing it in the Highlands. We sleep in a hotel, in a bed."

"Do you not see how these people look at us? They are fearful."

He watched Brenna scan the faces of people on the sidewalk. Some scurried into the closest building. Others frozen to the spot they stood, staring as they passed.

"Just smile and wave. We'll be fine," she said and sat up taller in the saddle.

###

Lachlan took her advice and practiced the 'smile and wave' approach to the horrified looks they garnered as they made their way to the inn. It was actually rather comical. He walked barefoot and his long raven hair wafted in his wake. Bare chested with a plaid that barely clung to his hips. He looked wild, imposing, and beautiful.

She limped along at his side as they entered the inn. The man behind the front desk stared at Lachlan, wide eyed and speechless.

"Oh. My. God. Honey, who *is* your friend? He looks like Conan the Barbarian. Be still my heart."

Brenna couldn't help the chuckle that bubbled from her lips. "We'd like a room for the night, if you have one available." She reached into her pocket and pulled out a wad of bills.

"Of course, of course, anything for *him*," he said, still staring at Lachlan, who promptly turned his back on the man. The clerk's eyes dropped to look at Lachlan's backside admiringly. He sighed and rolled his eyes with delight.

"Room twelve, second floor. Here's your key." He propped his elbows on the counter and rested his chin in his hands. The puppy dog eyes he gave Lachlan were over-the-top drama queenesque.

Brenna linked her arm through Lachlan's and led him to the elevator. A shock of heat flowed from where she touched his arm to pool in her belly. Her most private parts tingled. The doors opened with a *ding* the moment she pushed the call button. Lachlan tensed at the sight of the small, enclosed area.

"It's an elevator," she said and stepped in, pulling him along beside her. "It's very secure and will take us up to the floor where our room is located. We could have taken the stairs, but I thought this would be more fun." She pressed the button for the second floor and the doors whooshed shut. There was so much to show him.

Room twelve was much nicer than the room she'd had the previous night. Must be something to do with the desk clerk's admiration for Lachlan. This room was very blue. Blue paisley comforter, blue and white striped curtains, blue shag carpet, and fake blue roses in a white vase sat forlornly on the bedside table.

"What do you think has happened to Hafnar?" Brenna asked.

"Can't say for sure, but we both need rest, otherwise we won't stand a chance against him."

Lachlan's keen eyes scanned the room, taking in the amenities. He flicked the switch on the wall and the bedside lamp glowed with light. He flicked it off. On. Off. "Fascinating." He chuckled.

"How about something to eat? I'll order room service." He offered her a bemused smile.

"Aye. Steak and ale." He smoothed a hand over the bedspread and tested the mattress with his weight. A sigh escaped him as he settled into the softness.

Brenna placed their order and returned her attention to Lachlan. He beckoned to her with a pat on the mattress next to him. She gingerly sat beside him and found herself guided by strong arms onto his lap.

She leaned into his chest and welcomed his embrace. The steady beat of his heart lulled her. A moment later a hardness grew more apparent between his legs and his ragged kilt did nothing to confine his desire for her.

She was suddenly self-conscious of how disheveled her appearance must be. As bad as she thought she looked, it didn't seem to adversely affect the bulge that pushed more firmly on her backside.

She pulled away from him and lifted a hand to caress his cheek. She dropped her eyes to marvel at the fullness of his bottom lip, the prominent line of his chiseled cheekbones. His nose, straight and a tad too long to be deemed perfect. And those eyes. One could get lost in the depth of those eyes and never return. She hadn't been with a man in—a long damn time.

"Let me show you the bathroom. You can take a nice, hot shower while we wait for the food to be delivered." She jumped off his lap, her mouth suddenly dry. He followed her into the washroom.

The room was comfortably large, glaringly white, and not a claw footed tub in sight. Her stomach fluttered, and she reached for the shower knobs. "This one is for hot water, this one for cold. You can adjust them until you find a comfortable temperature. Let's see…this bottle here is shampoo, to wash your hair with. Here's the soap." She unwrapped the miniature bar for him. "And towels are over there." She pointed to the towel bar, then turned to make sure he didn't have any ques. . .tions. *Holy Mother of God.*

He stood before her naked, and glorious, and oh so very aroused. His tattered kilt lay on the floor at his feet.

Magnificent. She'd known he would be; bare-chested was one thing, but here, towering above her, eyes hooded with passion, he looked like the Faerie gods from whom he descended.

She threw her hands up to cover her eyes and felt the scorching heat of a five-alarm blush flush her cheeks. "I'll…I'll let you know when our food arrives." She dashed from the room, and Lachlan's baritone laughter rang out rich, warm, and amused. She closed the door behind her and leaned against the solid surface until her legs quit their quivering.

Her feet seemed to be drifting along on a cloud, and she floated over to the bedside. She plopped onto the king sized bed, smiling in contentment. Then she lost herself in thoughts. Pleasant, happy, dirty thoughts. Very dirty.

A knock on the door threw her violently out of her fantasy. The one starring her. And Lachlan. And a lot of exposed flesh.

She opened the door and Red Hair and Freckles walked in carrying a silver domed serving tray. He ignored her and scanned the room, presumably looking for Lachlan. The poor guy. His shoulders slumped in disappointment.

"That was fast," Brenna said.

Red walked to the small table and placed the tray next to the fake blue roses, then held out his hand. Brenna dug in her jeans pocket for a tip. Lachlan chose that moment to open the bathroom door and make an appearance. A blue towel hugged his lean hips and water dripped from his raven hair.

Red stuttered. "I-I brought your dinner." He beamed.

Brenna stuffed a five-dollar bill in his hand and said, "Thank you so much. That'll be all we need for now."

Red didn't move, just stared at Lachlan with his jaw hanging open. At least the guy had good taste. Brenna nudged him in the direction of the door. He finally collected himself and backed out of the room. His eyes never left Lachlan's physique, and the tent in the front of his khaki pants left no doubt of his opinion. She seconded the motion.

"Ye were right, lass. The shower is a wonderful invention. Hot water with the turn of a knob. Rather a spectacular idea." He seated himself at the table and lifted away the silver cover from the tray. Steam rose from the steak and a dollop of butter oozed over the edge. The chef's salad she ordered looked painfully boring, so she started with the Crème Brulee.

Lachlan savored every bite and groaned in delight with each swallow. Each rumble from his throat sent little shivers skittering to her core. He finished and leaned back in the chair, folding his hands over his stomach, and stretching out his legs, crossing them at the ankles. She picked at her salad, too nervous to eat anymore.

"I think I'll, ah, brush my teeth." She scampered from the table. Lachlan followed her into the bathroom.

"This is a toothbrush, and this is toothpaste." She handed him the brush and squirted out the blue gel onto the end of it. She proceeded to demonstrate its use and Lachlan mimicked her actions.

He cocked an eyebrow and seemed rather intrigued. Then he swallowed and wrinkled his nose and forehead. "*Blech*. That's nasty."

Brenna nearly choked and spit out a mouthful of toothpaste into the sink. "You don't swallow, you spit it out and rinse your mouth out with water." Laughter lilted from her.

"Next time, I'll watch from beginning to end when ye show me something new." He took her hand and led her to the bedroom. He sat on the edge of the bed and turned her, placing her on his lap. "Lass, there is something ye should know."

Brenna shifted in his lap. His hand moved from holding her body, to touching her face. He traced a finger along the ragged edge of her scar.

"Ye've come to mean a great deal to me, Brenna. Not because ye've freed me. Because of who ye are. Yer values. Yer bravery. Yer willingness to do the right thing. Ye've changed my life, forever. Now I intend to change yers."

She closed her eyes for a moment. Could he truly mean those words? It took a moment before she remembered to breathe.

He pulled her closer and pressed his lips to her forehead then tilted her chin back and kissed the tip of her upturned nose.

He barely brushed his lips against hers, seeking permission. Answering his unspoken question, she ran her fingers through his hair and traced the outline of his mouth with her tongue.

Brenna felt bereft when he pulled away and opened her eyes to search for the reason. She had little experience with men in these situations. Few had gotten past the knowledge of her psychic abilities and actually stuck around long enough to have a physical relationship. Curiosity mainly. They thought sleeping with a psychic would be different somehow. When they realized it wasn't, they moved on.

The encounters left her insecure and that threatened to ruin this moment with Lachlan. No. This was different. He was different. She knew him to his core. Sometimes life required an empty handed leap into the void, consequences be dammed. For this man, she would leap. She shifted her body and straddled his lap refusing to let him escape.

"Gods, lass. Ye take me breath away." He cupped her face with his hands. Heat skittered down her neck to her breasts and she ached for his touch.

She rocked forward, against the hardness pressing between her thighs. Desire smoldered in the green depths of his eyes. She held back nothing and kissed him. His mouth yielded to hers and parted for her tongue to entwine with his.

Rough hands chapped by the sea slid up the back of her sweater, and the blood pumped through her veins with the ferocity of a raging river. Gooseflesh rose on her skin where he touched her, and shivers raced up her spine.

He pulled her hips forward and back, forward and back, rocking her against him. A moan escaped her parted lips.

His hands reached for the hem of her sweater, lifting the wool over her head. Waves of hair spilled over her shoulders and he caressed her bare breasts. Bra's were so not her. Her nipples hardened in the coolness of the room.

He pressed his lips to the hollow space between her breasts and trailed his tongue to the place where her heart threatened to burst. He continued his trail up her throat, to her chin and then her lips. She pulled away, lifted her hair and wrapped the strands around her wrist to flip the coil across her back and out of his way.

An arm encircled her waist and he rolled her onto her back all the while his mouth ravished hers. His hands left her body long enough to flick his wrist, freeing him from his towel, tossing it onto a heap on the floor.

The cowboy boots he tugged off and tossed into the growing pile of discarded clothes. The fastenings of her jeans confounded him, and she reached for the zipper, pulled it down, and pushed the pants down to her thighs. He drew them past her knees and tossed them into a heap not far from his towel.

Her thighs parted from the subtle pressure of his knee. Holding his weight on his elbow, he didn't take his eyes from her. A wave of heat rose in her belly and her skin tingled with excitement.

A fire blazed along the path he traced with his fingers, down the nape of her neck to the hollow where it joined her shoulder. He drew a languid circle around her nipple and then a trail across her ribs to the hypersensitive expanse of skin from her belly to her hip. His touch traveled a meandering path until it reached between her tender folds and touched her nub. The circles he drew there with his fingers brought her to the edge of ecstasy. One finger, then two, slipped inside her core, stroking her, stretching her, preparing her to receive him. He lifted her hips with his free hand and paused at her entrance; his eyes never left hers.

"Are ye sure, lass? Because, if we go any farther, I don't think I can stop. There'll be no going back."

"Lachlan, I've never been more sure of anything. Don't stop. Please. Don't stop."

He pulled her closer and filled her slowly with his rigid length. She hadn't been with a man in a long time. And she'd never been with a man who stretched her body to fit him inside hers. It was glorious.

Inch by inch, he buried himself in her warmth. His mouth found her breast and his tongue traced around her nipple and he nipped the tender flesh with his teeth, she ground against him in response.

"Forgive me, lass, I can't be gentle this time," he whispered.

Brenna wrapped her legs around his waist and pulled him deeper inside her. She traced his bottom lip with the tip of her tongue.

He covered her mouth with his and began to move his hips in an ancient rhythm. Matching each of his strokes without hesitation, without restraint, she lost herself in the crescendo of voices roaring in her head.

The coil that had formed in her belly the first time she saw Lachlan tightened. Her breathing grew ragged and she flexed her muscles, tightening her sheath on his shaft. A tidal wave of sensation gave way and wracked her body. A cry of pleasure tore from her throat and her bones melted. Lachlan pressed his forehead against hers, watching as her body convulsed beneath him. His back bowed and he bellowed with his own release.

Lachlan lay propped on an elbow beside her, his leg thrown casually over her thighs, his hand covering a breast. A tiny sob escaped from her lips. Lachlan watched as a wayward tear slipped from the corner of her eye. His brows pinched together with concern and he caught the errant drop with a kiss.

"I'm sorry, lass, I didn't mean to hurt ye," he said. His voice cracked with emotion.

"You didn't. That was just so. . .can't believe we. . .I've never. . .been better in my entire life."

"Nor have I, lass," he said and enfolded her tightly into his arms and wrapped her with his body.

CHAPTER THIRTEEN

Lachlan kissed her eyelids and woke her. A contented smile slid across her face when his desire nudged against her thigh. Sparks flickered to a flame as he feathered kisses along the length of her neck. Slender fingers raked his hair and pulled him closer for a morning kiss.

Magnificent streaks of crimson ribboned through the window. Lachlan turned to witness the sunrise with wonderment and awe.

"I don't want to ever miss another daybreak, lass."

"I prefer sunsets. I don't have to get up early to enjoy them."

"Aye, lass. I've learned that about ye. A couple days and we'll be home to see one."

Loath to leave the warmth of his embrace, she reached for her sweater in the heap of discarded clothes on the floor. The bloody jeans, she rolled up and stuffed in the wastebasket and removed a new pair of red silk panties and jeans from the saddlebag that served as her suitcase.

"I almost forgot. Colin insisted I guesstimate your clothing size and bring these along for you." She set a pair of black jeans, a grey long sleeved tee, and sneakers on the end of the bed. "Might as well try them on. The scrap of cloth you call a kilt isn't going to last much longer."

"I'll have ye know that scrap of cloth was woven with Faerie magic and it will survive as long as I do." He sounded disgruntled.

Lachlan rose from the bed they'd shared, standing naked and glorious, he chuckled when he caught her staring. She blushed and dropped her eyes. When he turned his back, she took advantage of the situation and unashamedly got an eyeful of his backside before moving along on her intended course to the bathroom to freshen up.

When she returned, Lachlan was dressed. The shirt pulled too tightly across his chest, the pants were two inches too short, and he looked divine.

"How are the sneakers?" she asked.

He quirked an eyebrow. "Sneakers?"

"Shoes. Those particular shoes are called sneakers."

"Ah, I see. Too bloody small." He tugged at the thigh of the pants, pulling them down. "These trews are a bit. . . restrictive."

She chuckled at his meaning and said, "Give them a couple of hours in the saddle and they'll stretch."

They packed up the remainder of their meager belongings and walked to the elevator. Lachlan pushed the button to call it to their floor. He learned quickly.

The elevator doors whooshed open and an elderly couple stepped to the rear of the compartment. Once aboard, Lachlan pressed the button numbered two. The doors began to close then abruptly halted. "It's broken."

Brenna reached out and pressed the L-button and Lachlan grunted. The doors closed and they descended to the lobby. They headed out into the sunshine and rounded the corner of the B&B to retrieve Enbarr. Once saddled, seated, and out of town, the Fae horse set a fast pace in an easterly direction. They continued in relative silence, well past the noon hour, with only a short break for Brenna to walk a little and relieve her jostled bladder.

Lachlan waited for her return from the stand of trees that provided her some privacy. He shielded his eyes from the sun and scanned the sky. He turned in a small circle as he did so.

"What are you searching for?" Brenna asked.

"I'm looking to see if our friend still follows us. There he is, lass," Lachlan said, indicating the direction she should look.

"Oh my gosh, you're right. That is him. He's so far away, how will he manage to help keep us safe from that distance?"

"He keeps his distance to avoid being spotted and causing a panic. Those expansive wings move him quickly enough. His eyes are very keen, I would think. He'll know if any danger approaches."

Lachlan closed the few feet between them and swooped down so quickly to steal a kiss, she didn't see it coming. Her heart leapt in her chest and tingles spread from her lips to her toes and made her shiver with delight.

A glint of mischief turned his eyes a shade of freshly sprouted spring grass. She'd seen them clouded over with grief and sorrow and pain, hooded with passion, but mischief was a new and welcome emotion.

"Come now, lass, let's get moving. I've a mind to give Enbarr his head so we can make good time. If I recall correctly, we've a ways to go yet."

"Let me just check in with Colin. I want him to know we're all right." She pulled a satellite phone from one of the pouches attached to a saddlebag. "I should have called him yesterday, but you distracted me."

"What is that thing?"

"It's a satellite phone. When I dial the number of the person I want to call, it sends a signal to a satellite then transfers the signal to that person's phone. When they answer, we can talk."

"I don't understand what ye mean. Show me."

"You pull out this thing, the antenna, then on this particular phone, you press this button and the number one, and it will call Colin." She pushed the buttons as she explained and put the phone to Lachlan's ear.

"What do I do now?" he asked.

"When he answers, you talk to him."

Several moments passed in silence while the call connected. The twinkle of wonder flashed in Lachlan's eyes. "Hello."

A beat passed and Lachlan's eyes grew round. He turned to her and flashed her a dazzling smile. "Hello. Aye, this is Lachlan. Are ye well?" Lachlan shouted into the phone. The smile morphed into a smirk and he appeared quite pleased with his foray into the twenty first century. He assured Colin they were fine and that they were on their way home. He handed the phone back to her.

“To end the call, you press this button, otherwise the connection will continue and run up Colin’s bill.” She pushed the button and returned the phone to its pack. “And you should say ‘goodbye’ when you’re ready to end the call.”

Still grinning, he swung himself up effortlessly onto Enbarr. He lifted her up, setting her firmly behind him.

The days of hard riding, and other activities, had left certain body parts hideously sore. Lachlan fashioned her cloak into a makeshift pillow upon which to sit astride Enbarr. She smiled at the gesture and was pleased the ersatz cushion made a difference, at least initially.

Given free rein, Enbarr blazed over the highland terrain, and she didn’t distract Lachlan with conversation. Instead, she passed the time by keeping an eye on the dragon. He circled them from a great distance, fading in and out of view.

Several more hours into the journey and despite the speed, the constant pounding her body was taking in the saddle, she grew weary from the effort of keeping herself seated on Enbarr’s back. She longed to stop and grab a power nap, but remained silent. To keep Lachlan from his home any longer than necessary seemed cruel. They continued onward into the twilight.

Reflecting on the night before, Brenna’s chest filled with warmth. The intimacy they’d shared sent a ripple of gooseflesh scurrying down her arms and a coil tightened low in her belly. She wanted to be home, in his bed, with his body covering hers.

###

Soren descended in lazy circles and set down on the driveway outside the gatehouse, landing as light as a bird. The air shimmered and the man stood in the dragon’s stead.

Sliding from Enbarr's back until his feet touched the gravel drive, Lachlan breathed a heavy sigh of relief. Brenna slid into his arms. He couldn't resist kissing her.

The manor house door slammed open and a tall copper haired man strode toward them. Holding his arms wide, he embraced Brenna in welcome.

"Colin. I'm so glad to see you," she said.

Lachlan bit back a wave of unfair jealousy. Colin played nearly as large a role in his rescue as Brenna. He owed this man his gratitude.

Colin extended his hand in greeting. "It's about bloody well time I have the pleasure of meeting ye. Ye'll be welcome here as long as ye wish. Brenna, too, of course."

"I thank ye for the offer. I'm pleased that Highland hospitality has not gone out of style over the centuries. This is Soren. He is of the Draconian race. He stood with me against my brother, though Hafnar escaped our wrath. This time. Have ye a room for him as well?"

"Of course." Colin bowed slightly in respect of the ancient dragon man.

"I need a shower and a nap. I'll join you boys in a while," Brenna said and left them.

"Come. Let's get ye both something to eat. I think we could all use a whisky." Colin led the men into the B&B and motioned to the great hall table. "Sit. I'll be back with a bottle."

Lachlan settled in a chair and stretched out his legs. "Soren, I thank ye for seeing us safely home." The dragon man nodded once and settled in the chair across from him.

Colin returned and poured three glasses of the burnished bronze liquid. "It's The Glenlivit, aged eighteen years. Stew's heating on the stove."

Lachlan swirled the vessel and watched slow legs run down the side of the glass. His nose detected butter, lemon, and a hint of sweet honey. The scents made his mouth water. One gulp and the last vestiges of ice melted from his bones and kindled a warm fire in his belly.

Colin poured him another.

This glass, he sipped slowly and savored. "Ye prepared her well, Colin. I thank ye for helping her. For helping me. My debt to ye is great."

"Nonsense. That ye are a free man is all the payment I could want." Colin lifted his glass. "A toast, to freedom, and new beginnings." They *clinked* glasses and tossed back their drinks.

"What will ye do now, Lachlan?" Colin asked. He poured a third round.

"I'll not rest until I have my brother's head. I'll not have him threatening me or Brenna anymore. The first thing I shall do is find my sister and father. They will search for him in Faerie and we can search for him here, that is, if yer willing." Lachlan paused, hoping the men would assist him.

Soren was the first to speak. "I have equal reason to want Hafnar dead. I am with you."

Colin grimaced and narrowed his eyes. "The portals to Faerie were sealed by yer father centuries ago. Yet, you think there is a need to search for him here?"

Lachlan nodded in the affirmative. "He's visited me in the cavern a number of times over the years. He's tried to kill Brenna by tossing her off a cliff and drowning her in the bath. Even one as powerful as he cannot accomplish those things from the Fae realm. He was here. Could be here still."

Colin flinched and shook his head, disbelieving. "So somewhere, there is an open portal. Has been for years. Son of a bitch. If I'd have known I'd have searched out a full blooded Fae to cross and bring word to yer father." Colin kicked back his chair and paced the room. "Fuck. I have failed ye, Lachlan." His nostrils flared and his face reddened. He grabbed his drink off the table, tossed back his fourth round of scotch and hurled the glass at the fireplace shattering it against the stone hearth.

Silence descended and each man beat back the demons in their own minds. Lachlan stood and marched from the room, out the front door and into the yard. Colin and Soren glanced at each other, then followed.

Lachlan bent down and selected a small rock from the driveway. He rolled it between his thumb and forefinger. "When my sister and I were children, I spent most of my time in this realm. Humans are forbidden in Faerie. Any who chance to cross to the Fae realm are marked for death. As a half-fae prince, I was an exception and was allowed some time with my family. My sister and I were quite close. We would use Seer stones to communicate between our worlds. The stones we used were unimportant. The power did not lie with them, but with each of us. If I focus my mind on the center of the stone and think about the person I wish to see, they'll appear, and we'll be able to see and speak with one another. Ariel would wear her stone around her neck. Of course, that was many lifetimes ago, but worth a try."

Colin and Soren moved closer and Lachlan cupped his hand and brought the stone to rest in his palm. He focused his thoughts and energy to its center. The stone glowed from within, a tiny moon in the palm of his hand. The colors of the rainbow appeared and swirled like storm clouds. Suddenly, all color vanished, cleared like the mist of a Highland morning. Except for one.

Lachlan had forgotten his sister's affection for purple. Violet colored lace hung from the four posters of the bed in which she slept. Midnight hair was strewn over her pillow, the only white object in the room. The orchid comforter concealed her alabaster skin from her neck to her toes.

Ariel sat up and grasped the stone suspended from her neck by an intricate gold chain. She peered into the stone and could form no words.

"My wee faerie mouse, ye look more beautiful than the day I saw ye last. I've missed ye, Mouse," Lachlan said.

Ariel gasped and tears welled in her eyes and cascaded down her face in twin rivers. A faerie dragon poked its snout out from the blankets and sniffed the air. The creature waddled from her nesting spot and settled into Ariel's lap to offer comfort by cooing and licking her hand. "Is it truly you, brother?" Ariel choked on a sob.

"Aye." God he'd missed her.

CHAPTER FOURTEEN

Lachlan made his way to the great hall with a determined jaunt in his step. He'd slept horizontally, in a soft bed with a beautiful woman, for whom he cared deeply. He'd talked with his sister for the first time in more than half a millennium, and she was searching Faerie for Hafnar and an open portal. She would send word to their father, who was away at court, to return home immediately. Soon, his brother would surface, and when he did, justice would be swift and unmerciful.

"Any sign of Hafnar during the night?" Lachlan asked.

"Not yet. He might still be licking his wounds," Soren said.

"Hrmph. More likely he's waiting for an opportunity." Lachlan seated himself at the head of the table and grabbed a plateful of bacon and eggs.

"Then perhaps we should provide him with one?" Colin suggested.

"Elaborate on that thought." The bacon crunched, and he closed his eyes, savoring the morsel.

"Well, why wait on him to determine the next move. What if we draw him out, bait him if ye will. Put you and Brenna in a position of weakness and when he thinks he's found his opportunity, we'll be there to greet him," Colin said.

"The plan has merit. I want the matter settled posthaste." Lachlan leaned back in his chair, crossing his ankles. "What say ye, Soren?"

"I'll not be free until Hafnar's met his fate. I'll never rid myself of the stink of that dank cavern. I say we've nothing to lose by trying such a plan."

"I don't fear for myself, but putting Brenna at risk is not something I take lightly," Lachlan said.

"She has spunk. And brains. And she did save our sorry asses," Soren said with a wink.

"Ah, yer bloody right. It's just—I've only just found her."

Soren leaned forward, clapping Lachlan on the shoulder. "I only hope that I have half as much luck finding myself as fine a woman as she. We'll keep her safe."

Lachlan nodded thoughtfully. "I'm taking breakfast up to Brenna. I trust ye'll have the details settled when I return." He pushed his chair from the table, took a plateful of food with him and strode to the stairs.

He paused outside his chamber door, his heightened Fae hearing picked up the sound of Brenna's humming on the other side. It pleased him. He balanced the plate in one hand and swung open the door.

Brenna's wet hair hung unbound down her back, and her cheeks blossomed with a blush. A fresh change of clothes outlined her curves, and the colored toes she was so fond of peeked out beneath her cuffed pants. She was exquisite. A shy smile tilted the corners of her perfect pink lips, and he found himself with a raging hard on.

"I've brought ye a bit to eat." He set the dish on an antique writing table. A fresh breeze wafted in from the nearby window. "Come, sit and eat." He pulled out the chair for her and waited while she put her hairbrush down on the night table. She sat and dug in.

"Mmmmm. I'm starving. I'm not used to being awake half the night—you know, not sleeping." Her color deepened.

Lachlan took the brush from the nightstand and stood behind her. "May I?"

Brenna looked over her shoulder, and her grey eyes danced with a shimmer of blue. She nodded and returned her attention to her plate.

The mass of auburn weighed heavy in his hand. Carefully, he brushed the silken strands free of tangles, and the heavenly scent of lavender brought peace to his soul.

"My mother would brush my hair dry when I was a little girl. I think it's the fondest memory I have of her. She stopped right after I started hearing the voices in my head. I don't think she's touched me since that day. No kisses, no hugs, no being tucked into bed. It broke my heart."

"Aye. I know the pain ye speak of. There were many things I missed while in the cavern." He tugged gently at a knot in her hair, running his fingers through the length of it. "It's hard to say which pained me most."

"Tell me," she whispered. She stood and turned, taking his hand, she led him to the chair and sat him down. She folded herself onto the floor in front of him and waited for him to speak.

Unsure where to begin, he leaned forward and breathed in the scent of her. "I missed the smell of lavender, and rain, and peat burning on the hearth. The sound of the wind and the chatter of birds. Searching the sky for falling stars and watching the constellations change with the seasons. I couldn't remember the colors of gloaming, or the taste of rabbit stew, or oysters fresh from the sea. And whisky. I missed fine Scotch whisky."

Brenna rose to her knees and touched his lips tracing their outline with her finger. She explored the line of his jaw, down the length of his neck across the linen of his shirt to his shoulder, down his arm, all the way to the tip of his finger. She turned his hand over and placed a kiss in his palm.

"Aye, I missed touch most of all. I will never get enough of ye touching me, lass."

He captured her face in his hands and slanted his lips over hers. His heart raced and longing raged in his loins again. Still. Her lips parted and welcomed home his ravaged heart.

Only when she pulled away did he hear the incessant banging on the door. He released his hands from her face and rested his forehead against hers. He kissed the tip of her nose and rose from the chair. She jumped up from the floor and sank onto the seat Lachlan vacated.

"It bloody well better be important," he shouted to the knocker.

He opened the door with more vigor than necessary causing the hinges to creak under the strain. Colin and Soren ducked under the arm he braced against the jamb and strode into the room.

"Hope we're not interrupting anything," Soren said, mischief etched all over his face.

"Ye were. Now, what is it that couldn't wait?"

"We've a plan worked out and came to see if Brenna was feeling up to catching a vile Faerie," Soren said.

Brenna peeked around the chair. "I'm in. What are we doing?"

###

The sun tried in vain to burn away the thick cover of clouds dancing with the breeze across the dove grey sky. Enbarr pulled the cart upon which she and Lachlan sat over the last undulating hill and brought them within range of the one entrance to Lachlan's ruined castle. Lachlan refused to let her drive them over in the Cooper, but promised he'd learn a few things about driving in the coming days. Apparently, he thought her driving skills were lacking and reminded her of the sheep she'd nearly run down. Besides, the wagon provided needed cover for their plan.

Colin had drawn the short straw and left the B&B before dawn and spent the final hours of night hidden in the ruined castle. His task was to help protect them in the event Hafnar took the bait. By now, he would be waiting for them with a quiver of deadly iron arrows slung over his shoulder and a lethal crossbow in his hand. Implements of Faerie destruction. Brenna caught a glimpse of Colin. He wore a cape of sorts woven from the highland grasses to conceal his presence once in the open. Camouflage paint caked his face and arms, completing the savage ensemble.

Answerer lay docile under the cover of a blanket on the floorboard of the cart, though when she reached her hand towards its slumbering spot, it hummed and its magic flowed through her fingers. Lachlan had hidden two sgian dhubhs, black daggers, at her waist, but she missed the weight of the ancient sword on her person.

Several hundred yards later, Lachlan tugged the reins and halted Enbarr. He loped around the back of the cart and wrapped powerful hands around her middle, then lifted her from her seat as if she weighed no more than a kitten. She glanced over his shoulder and looked for Colin who should be crawling on his belly to within cross bow range. He'd vanished into the grasses with the stealth of a ghost.

Lachlan gathered the blanket from the floorboard, the Answerer still concealed within its folds, and Brenna grabbed the picnic basket from the rear of the wagon. They carefully laid out the bedspread, unpacked lunch, and appeared to settle in for a lazy afternoon.

"Well, so far so good," Brenna said. She crossed her legs pretzel style and snatched an apple from the basket.

Lachlan unsheathed his own dagger and sliced off a chunk of the fruit. He handed her a piece, then sliced another for himself.

"You know, the one part of this plan that we didn't discuss is what we're going to do with Hafnar when we capture him," she said.

A frown formed between his eyebrows, and his gaze pinned her to the spot. "I thought it would be obvious, lass. I intend to kill him."

Brenna felt the blood drain from her face. "You can't kill him."

"The hell I can't. After what he's done? He's left me no choice." His voice deepened and his nostrils flared.

She tried again. “Isn’t there some sort of Faerie court that he should be turned over to?”

“Nay. I’ll not do him that courtesy.”

“But he’s your brother.”

“He’s my enemy. Our enemy.”

“All the more reason why you aren’t a fair and impartial judge.” Brenna wrung her hands.

“Lass, I don’t give a fuck about fair or impartial. The man kept me in a cavern for centuries, and he’ll pay for that with his bloody life.”

“Don’t you think you’ll find it hard to live with, killing your own flesh and blood?” she asked. The thought of blood and guts being shed before her eyes unsettled her stomach.

“Nay. I don’t see a problem.”

“I wish you’d reconsider—”

“Lass, he is yer enemy as well as mine. He threatens both our lives as long as he is alive.”

Brenna picked through the basket and looked for the bottle of wine she’d pilfered from Colin’s collection. The hour was early to start drinking, but this conversation was shaping up to be their first fight, and she needed a bit of bolstering.

She was silent for a few minutes while she uncorked the bottle. “Say that you’ll think about turning him over.”

“I could say such, but it would be an untruth.”

“Say it anyway,” Brenna said and took a swig sans a glass.

Lachlan scrubbed his face with his hand and shook his head in exasperation. She handed him the bottle. He scowled at her and she thought she’d pushed him too far.

"Bloody hell, lass. All right, I'll consider letting Hafnar live."

"Good." Her shoulders dropped several inches with relief. "Because here he comes."

A speck circled high above and wove a path through the clouds. The black dragon and its rider kept their distance and appeared to weigh possibilities; no doubt they searched for hidden danger. The air whooshed from her lungs when Lachlan lunged for her and pulled her down across his body in a lovers embrace. All the while, he looked to the sky for their enemy. Brenna played along with the ploy and riddled him with feather light kisses, trailing them across the underside of his neck.

"What's he doing?" she whispered.

"Still circling, closer now," he said and rolled over on top of her. He tossed his shirt into the grass, keeping up the charade.

"I see him." She raked her hands over his broad back and wrapped her legs around his waist. "He has no idea this is a setup."

"Try to keep an eye on him, lass, while I pretend to be distracted." He wagged his eyebrows at her and covered her lips with his. She tried, she really did, but the moment his tongue slipped between her teeth and tickled the roof of her mouth, Hafnar disappeared behind her closed lids.

"Bloody hell, yer supposed to be watching him." He flipped her from beneath him and dropped her astride his hips. "He's coming in, fast and low over the castle hill. He thinks we're here for a good tupping." He reached under the blanket and grasped the hilt of the Answerer. The air hummed with the dragon's approach. The direction of Hafnar's attack spoiled their carefully laid plan. The man in the grass could not let loose his iron arrows without risk of harm to the two of them.

Lachlan's battle cry rent the air, and Brenna rolled off him and away. He rose, sword in hand, and lunged for the belly of the dragon as it soared just out of reach. Soren flew from the back of the cart, bits of hay clung to him, and he too was armed with a crossbow.

"Take him alive," Lachlan shouted.

Soren hesitated at the command and aimed his bow. "Feck, no," he bellowed.

"No, Soren!" Brenna pleaded at the top of her lungs. The arrow flew and impaled the black dragon's hindquarter, missing Hafnar by a goodly amount. A scream of pain tore from the beast, and a stream of blood flowed from the wound like rain. Hafnar faltered in the saddle and gestured wildly with his hands in the air, a furious look upon his face. He cast a lightning bolt from his fingertips. Flames exploded, but didn't catch. Flickers of fire singed the ground near their picnic blanket, but nothing more.

The dragon pulled up. Bat-like wings beat the air and carried Hafnar out of range.

Tendrils of smoke puffed from Soren's nostrils and curled wisplike around his face. Clenched fists and pursed lips sent Brenna fleeing to stand behind Lachlan, afraid Soren would torch her where she stood if she didn't get out of his line of fire.

"Our man-dragon is really pissed," she said and pressed herself against Lachlan's back.

"Aye, he is. Walk with me, Soren," Lachlan said and strode forward to lead him away from her.

Colin, still draped in woven grass approached her and stood watch while they waited for Soren and Lachlan to return. And waited. And waited some more.

Laughter preceded them, and Soren called out for Brenna. She stepped closer to Colin. A nod from Lachlan reassured her. He had resolved the matter with Soren.

"That was a brilliant idea you had, Brenna," Soren said. He took her hand and bowed slightly in respect.

Baffled by his reaction, she merely smiled and said, "Thank you. I'm glad you approve."

Brenna hung back with Lachlan while the others walked to the wooden cart. "What the hell did you tell him?"

A wicked grin broke across his face, "I told him ye thought to capture Hafnar alive, then we could torture him a bit, break a few bones, and cut off an appendage or two. Then, once he'd suffered appropriately, we'd eviscerate the bastard, then stake him with iron and watch him die."

"I didn't say that, I—"

"I know what ye said, lass, but I'd let the dragon believe otherwise for now. I wasn't the only one imprisoned in that bloody cavern."

They settled into the cart, and Enbarr took them home to Colin's B&B where they would work on plan B. Damn. They'd been so close.

###

The men returned to the B&B in a somber mood, disappointed, no doubt, their plan had gone awry. They broke open a new bottle of Scotch and lamented while they tossed about new ideas for capturing Hafnar.

Brenna left them to their scheming and wandered from room to room. The library beckoned, and she heeded the call. Dark mahogany shelves lined the walls from floor to ceiling. Each one gloriously overfilled, many of them double stacked. She ran her hand along the spines and stopped at random, pulling a book off the shelf. *Pride and Prejudice* by Jane Austin. She flipped through the first few pages and the distinct smell of old pages soothed her. The book was an autographed first edition. How odd that it designated Colin as the recipient. Must have been a different Colin. His great grandfather, perhaps. A first edition would have come out two centuries ago.

Holding the book like a prize, she decided to curl up on the couch and settle in for the afternoon. It would be hours yet before the men tired of planning their next move.

Colin's voice startled her awake from her cat nap. "Miss Sinclair, how are ye holding up, lass?" He sat on the couch next to her and draped his arm along the back of the couch.

"Well, I'm fine, actually."

"Hrmph. Well then, come with me. There's something I want to show you." He stood and headed for the door. She followed behind like an obedient puppy.

It was a short walk down the hall past Colin's private quarters. He stopped and unlocked a door and swung it open. "It's been quite a few years since I've been up here. Ye'll have to excuse the dust."

Round and round they climbed the stairs of this second tower room. The room at the top was an exquisite master suite. A distinct Victorian feel was evident in the flowered wallpaper, and the curves and scrollwork of the painted white furniture. Delicate lace hung from the windows and lush carpets littered the wood floor.

"I shared this space with my wife, before she—died." Colin ran a hand through his hair and shifted his weight from one leg to the other.

"Colin, I'm so sorry." He turned away and strode to a towering armoire.

"This is what I wanted to show you." He swung open the closet doors and pulled out two of the most elegant gowns she'd ever seen. "I thought we'd all share a nice meal this evening. A welcome home of sorts for Lachlan. I thought perhaps one of these might fit ye."

"Oh, Colin I couldn't possibly wear one of those. They belonged to your wife—I couldn't."

"I see. Well, it's yer choice. I just thought perhaps ye'd like something pretty to wear. My wife is long gone. It seems a shame to let her gowns hang here unloved and languishing. If ye care to reconsider, I'd be honored if ye wore one this evening."

For some reason, this seemed important to Colin. "I think the blue one would bring out my eyes, don't you?" she asked as she ran her hands down the plush velvet.

"Aye, it would. See if it fits. There's a changing screen over there." He pointed to the partition.

She scooped up the gown and hurried to try it on. The clip clap of Colin's boots told her he paced.

Brenna stepped out from behind the divider and ran her hands down the bodice of the gown. "Do I look all right?"

"Aye, ye look like a faerie princess. Lachlan will be quite pleased. Here, turn around and let me help with those blasted little buttons down the back." Colin's fingers were surprisingly nimble and he had her buttoned up in no time.

The full length mirror was mounted in silver, its edges encrusted with jewels of every shape and color reflected her countenance. The past few days spent outside fostered an outcropping of freckles across her nose and along her high cheekbones. Colin had been right; she did look like a princess. Except for the scar that arced across her cheek. She ran her fingers over its raised edges, remembering the failure that had earned her the mark.

"Is it crazy for me to fantasize about a happily ever after for Lachlan and me? I mean, he's a faerie prince and I'm a run-of-the-mill psychic. You know, scratch that I barely know him. I'm being an idiot." She dropped her gaze to the floor and thought her cowboy boots presented an interesting contrast to the elegant gown.

Colin lifted her chin with a finger. "Yer not an idiot, Brenna. I fell in love with my wife the moment I laid eyes on her. She was my mate. My partner. My one true love. It *is* possible to feel what ye do even after so short a time. Ye must embrace every moment ye have with him. Don't fret over yer differences. Celebrate them." He placed a chaste kiss on the top of her head. "Now, let's find shoes to match that gown." He turned from her and selected soft-soled silver slippers veined with gold thread. "See if these will do."

Brenna kicked off her boots and slipped on the shoes. Snug, but doable. Colin offered her his arm and she obliged. He led her down the tower stairs and her dress *swished* as she walked the hallway towards the great room. Butterflies fluttered in her stomach.

Embrace every moment.

Once they reached the threshold of the room, the butterflies shifted into woodpeckers and had a field day with her insides. Fresh bouquets of flowers stood in vases down the center of the great hall table. Old fashioned torches blazed in wrought iron holders along the walls casting shadows that danced along the Scotch pine floor. Wood piled in the fireplace awaited a flame and the soft strains of a waltz played from some concealed source.

Lachlan and Soren conversed by a tall arched window. Their conversation abruptly halted when Lachlan caught sight of them. He elbowed Soren, and Brenna swore a wisp of smoke escaped Soren's nostrils. She smiled at the silent compliment and hope Lachlan found her equally attractive.

Lachlan covered the distance of the room in a few impossibly long strides. Brenna curtsied formally and flashed him her most dazzling smile.

He reached for her hand and kissed her fingers. His eyes boldly admired her curves, enhanced by the clingy fabric of her indigo gown. Brenna tucked her arm through his and he escorted her to the dining table.

"I've never seen anyone more lovely then ye are this evening, lass," Lachlan said, as he took Brenna's hand and entwined his fingers with hers.

"Thank you," she said as the heat rose in her cheeks. "You're rather dashing yourself."

His long hair no longer hung down his back, but was cut to just below his shoulders. A fine white shirt covered his muscled chest and a new plaid in his clan colors of red and blue hung from his narrow waist. He looked regal and dashing and seeing him sent tingles to her toes. Soft black leather boots covered his calves and she fisted her hands with the effort to keep her insides from quivering.

Lachlan pulled out a chair for her and saw her seated. Soren had already made himself comfortable and poured them each a glass of wine.

Colin disappeared momentarily and returned with two platters of food.

"I understand these are yer favorite, Lachlan" Colin set down plates of oysters on the half shell. "There's rabbit stew simmering on the stove. I'll bring it out once these have disappeared." He gestured to the laden dishes.

Lachlan squeezed Brenna's hand. He raised his cup of wine, and his voice rang out clearly. "A toast to friends and freedom and love," he said as his eyes met Brenna's.

Glasses clinked in unison.

The oysters were to die for, only hours out of the sea. In mere minutes they'd disappeared and Colin served the rabbit stew. It tasted like chicken, but gamier. They ate well and laughed much throughout the dinner, and Brenna found that the wine tasted better after the third pour.

A bit giddy, she lost herself in the sounds of the music and imagined herself gliding across the floor in a formal waltz, twirling with the grace of a classically trained ballerina in the arms of her highland laird.

Lachlan turned to her with hooded eyes. "Dance with me, lass."

He'd been eavesdropping on her thoughts. "Do you know how to waltz?"

"I'm afraid not, lass."

"I'll teach you." She felt her face flush with excitement as Lachlan took her hand and led her to an open area of the room.

Brenna, insecure and not wanting to make a spectacle of herself in front of the men, pulled Lachlan along by the hand and continued walking through the stone arch on the far side of the room and out into the night.

"I thought we were going to dance, lass?" Lachlan said with disappointment in his voice.

"We are, but not in there. I thought I could show you out here, in private," she replied.

A smile replaced the disappointment on his face. She placed his arm around at her waist, taking his left hand in her right. He pulled her closer, squeezing the air out from between them. She didn't correct him. She stepped slowly from side to side, and he cocooned her in his embrace.

"Okay, this isn't exactly waltzing, this is swaying."

"Well then, I like this better," he said and winked at her, amusement dancing in his eyes.

A shiver rippled down her spine and goose flesh rose on her arms. The hair rose on the back of her neck and her breath hitched when he looked at her.

She stood unmoving in his arms. She was sure she was going to say something, but there didn't seem to be a thought in her head. His eyes never left hers as he began to move with her. The sound of the music drifted from the hall, lively with a quick beat. She ignored the melody. Didn't hear the notes over the sound of blood pulsing in her ears. They moved to their own rhythm. To the sound of a heartbeat.

He lowered his lips to hers. He tasted of wine, smooth and rich with a touch of berries.

She slipped her hand behind his neck and stood on her toes pulling him closer. Her lips parted and her tongue danced in tune with his. Her teeth scraped his bottom lip and a sound she didn't recognize escaped her throat. Passion bloomed in her belly and the hard length of him pressed against her.

He moved his hands along the curve of her back and held her to him. Her knees gave way, and she slid toward the ground. She melted, liquid and molten, and burned at his touch. He caught her below her knees and swung her up and into his arms, then carried her inside and took the stone stairs two at a time. His eyes never left hers.

In their room, the peat fire flickered in the stone fireplace and lavender scented candles filled the air with fragrance. Lachlan stood her on her feet at the edge of his bed. His lips crushed hers and he fumbled with the tiny buttons running down the back of her dress.

He mumbled a curse and smiled wickedly as he rent the remaining buttons from their material home, and she heard the suicidal jump of each one as they hit the stone floor and rolled to their deaths. She stiffened.

"Not to worry, lass. A bit of magic and the dress will be good as new."

She relaxed, and he slid her gown off her shoulders, traced the curve of her neck with velvety kisses and caressed her arms with his fingertips. She quivered with ripples of pleasure and gasped for a breath.

He urged the gown lower over her rounded hips. It slipped free and puddled at her feet. He pushed her hips back and sat her on the bed. Kneeling before her, he kissed a trail from her thighs to her knees. He pulled off her shoes and ran his finger across the sole of her foot. Her toes curled at the tickle. He trailed his tongue up the inside of her calf and licked lazy circles along the inside of her thigh.

She ran her fingers through his silken hair, and a gasp of pleasure escaped her lips.

He parted her knees, and when he kissed the most tender part of her womanhood, she cried out and dug her nails into his shoulders leaving half-moon imprints on his flesh.

She pulsed beneath his lips, hot and wet. A fire smoldered in the center of her body and ravaged her senses. He hastily threw off his kilt, drew the shirt over his head, and tossed it to the floor. He unlaced his leather boots in seconds and added them to the pile.

Her breath caught in her throat at the sight of his desire, and a brief moment of panic broke her revelry. Well-endowed did not begin to describe him. He shifted her to the center of his bed and lay beside her. His mouth ravished a breast while his hand worked magic on her hardened bud. Her stomach tightened, and she clenched her teeth. Her breath hitched, and her body wracked with release.

Two tiny tears slid from her eyes, and he caught one with a kiss.

"Why the tears, lass?"

"That was just. . .amazing."

"Aye, and the night is still young. I hope ye've rested well." His mouth tilted up in a wide grin broke across his face.

She slid a leg over his middle and straddled her immortal Highlander. His hardness stirred beneath her, and she slid his shaft inside her.

"It'll be you that needs resting when morning comes." She arched her back and rocked her hips in a slow, tortuous rhythm.

CHAPTER FIFTEEN

Brenna had no idea of the time when the first touches of awareness tickled her mind awake. She lay still in the bed she shared with Lachlan and listened for signs he was awake. Slow rhythmic breaths assured her he still slept, holding her close.

The few lovers she'd taken in her life never spent the night. She'd always awoken alone. A contented sigh and a long stretch made her smile and think of the Cheshire Cat. She certainly had something to smile about. Lachlan was extraordinary, and her feelings for the man stunned her. They made love into the early morning, and her body felt well used and pleasantly exhausted, but her mind was as wide awake as a child on Christmas morning.

Her thoughts wandered, and she imagined what Christmastime would be like here at the B&B with

Lachlan. It would be grand. Fresh pine boughs layered in the center of the great hall table. Candles and torches throwing amber light and a fire blazing on the hearth. A colossal Scotch pine tree, filling the air with its winter scent.

Lachlan tightened his grip on her and interrupted her musings. "Good morning to ye, lass. Did ye rest well?" His voice was husky with the first moments of wakefulness.

Her stomach fluttered at the rich sound. He propped himself up on his elbow and traced an invisible pattern across her chest with his finger. Gooseflesh rose on her arms and across her midsection. Lachlan dropped his head and ran his tongue around her nipple, cupping her breast in his hand.

"How about I bring ye some breakfast so we can stay here and spend the day the same as we spent the night?"

"I'd love it. I'm starved."

He retrieved his shirt from the floor and dug in the trunk at the foot of the bed settling on a pair of black leather pants. She watched, fascinated as he laced them up the front. The leather looked butter soft and did little to hide the shape of his muscular legs or his half hard member. Good Lord, was she doomed to want him every second for the rest of her days? And those days were numbered. She'd have to return home soon. But not just yet.

He threw more peat on the fire, all the while her eyes watched every movement he made with wanting in her heart.

"I won't be gone long, lass. Keep yer side of the bed warm will ye now?"

"Don't make me start without you," she said, and a flush of heat rose to her cheeks.

His laughter echoed in the stone stairwell. She snuggled under the covers and closed her eyes for a catnap.

###

Lachlan wasn't in the mood to be detained and set a course straight for the kitchen. Colin's voice rang out before he was even within sight of the great room where he and Soren ate breakfast.

He would spare a moment for his friend. He owed him a great debt for his part in helping the woman who was now in his bed keeping it warm for him. He owed him indeed.

"A bit late to rise this morning Lachlan, something keep you?" he said, teasing.

"Aye, a beautiful red-haired lass kept me busy, and ye know that well enough." Better he just admit it and get the teasing out of the way so he could return to Brenna.

Colin's teasing halted and he furrowed his brows, his face intent.

"What is it Colin? Is something amiss?" he asked.

He pressed a palm against his temple and closed his eyes.

Brenna's blood curdling scream broke the silence and sent rivers of ice through Lachlan's veins.

Soren toppled the chair where he sat, and the three men raced for the stairwell together.

Lachlan led the way ahead of Soren and Colin and took the stairs three at a time. He burst through the chamber door and scanned the room.

It was empty.

Lachlan placed his hand on the still warm spot where he'd left Brenna just minutes before. He'd left her alone. Unguarded. Unprotected.

Fuck. Hafnar waited for just such a moment and snatched her.

Colin joined them in the chamber. "How did the bastard get by us? There are wards all around us."

Soren looked out one of the large arched windows of the room, pointing to something in the distance. "He flew on the back of a dragon and came down from the roof. Looks like whoever set the wards needs a lesson, because they failed miserably in keeping Hafnar out."

The morning clouds shrouding the sky broke in the distance, and they watched the dragon disappear beyond the horizon, two riders upon its back.

"Brenna must be terrified," Colin said.

"Ye know Hafnar the best of the three of us, Lachlan. Where will he take her?" Soren asked.

"I don't have any idea where he would take her."

Lachlan fisted his hands in his hair and paced the length of the room. "Soren, if yer willing, we'll fly the skies in pursuit. Colin take Enbarr and keep up as best ye can. I'll contact my sister. She can watch for them in Faerie. Colin, have ye more of those gadgets with the buttons—what did Brenna call it?"

"Satellite phones? Aye, I'll get them and meet ye at the stable." Colin left them at a run and barreled down the stairs.

Hafnar had a head start and flew on the back of a dragon. It would be difficult, but not impossible for Enbarr to close the gap on the ground with his preternatural speed. Where was he taking her?

He couldn't lose the woman who'd freed his body and mind from the prison Hafnar created for him, the woman who'd stolen his heart.

He loved her.

It was his turn now, to save her.

Lachlan contacted Ariel through the Seer stone and updated her on what had transpired, then he and Soren headed for the stables.

Lachlan scanned the sky above and the first drops of rain, cold and heavy, fell free from the clouds, pelting them, as they hastened to the stables. Soren stopped outside the stable door and shifted to his dragon form.

Enbarr paced in his stall, running circles along the inside of his pen, tail whipping up and down swatting at some invisible enemy.

Lachlan threw the saddle over one arm and opened the gate to the stall with the other. Enbarr halted in front of him and stood still as the Reaper while being saddled.

Colin tossed Lachlan a phone then threw himself upon Enbarr's back. "The sword and the cloak are in that trunk, along with the breastplate. Take them." In a flourish of movement, Enbarr burst through the stable door into the pounding rain.

Anyone watching would question what they saw. A blur of motion, gone in a flash, with the observer left to question if they'd seen anything other than a swirl of mist on a dismal Highland morning.

Lachlan opened the wooden chest outside Enbarr's stall and removed the two items his clan had kept safe for him through the centuries of his exile. The Cloak of Invisibility and the Answerer. Brenna had used these artifacts to secure his freedom. He hoped they were enough to get her back. A third relic, the breastplate of Mannan Mac Lir, had been found and purchased by Colin just days ago. He donned the breastplate and slung the sword at his waist. How could he have left her alone? In the small span of time Brenna had been gone, his world felt completely amiss; life without her was unbearable. Another prison of Hafnar's making, this one infinitely worse than the one from which Brenna had freed him. He hastened outside to Soren.

Lachlan stared at the dragon's back. He waved his hands and fashioned a saddle large enough to span the back of the beast. Another wave and saddlebags filled with rations and necessities appeared. "I hope ye don't take offense to being saddled my friend." He hauled himself onto Soren's back. "Let's ride," he said, and Soren ascended to the sky, wings whooshing soundlessly as they climbed.

Lachlan.

He sat straight up on Soren, nearly unseating himself, and extended his mind to hers, listening.

He heard nothing but the din of splattering rain.

She'd reached for him, whispered his name, he was sure of it. Why hadn't she maintained the connection?

Lightening cleaved the sky and Lachlan searched for any sign of the black dragon and its riders.

Nothing.

###

Brenna struggled to stay alert. Hafnar kept forcing her to drink some concoction that made her want to sleep for a hundred years. They hadn't even left the tower room of MacGregor B&B before she fell limp into his embrace. She shivered at the memory of being held in his arms and shook her head as if she could erase his foul touch.

The potion rendered her incoherent for a while, though how long exactly she didn't know. Her first thought was of Lachlan. When the fog in her mind cleared, she had opened her eyes for a single blink and discovered tightly knotted ropes held her firmly in place on the back of a dragon. Hafnar was seated behind her, and they flew high above the ground.

Muddled thoughts like pieces of a puzzle formed and reformed in her hazed mind.

Hafnar.

He awakened her from her slumber in Lachlan's bed and stood glaring at her like some sick bastard. She'd screamed.

Fucking bastard.

Twice more she extended her mind to Lachlan. Had she reached him? Surely, he knew she'd been taken. Stirring from her position turned out to be a bad idea. Each time she did, Hafnar loosened the bindings enough to lift her back against his chest and forced more vile liquid down her throat leaving her oblivious in seconds.

Don't struggle and don't move. Don't struggle and don't move. Don't...

When next she woke, the air had stilled, no longer rushing past her. Silence replaced the sound of whooshing wings. A chill rippled over her skin, but she dared not shiver. A deep breath uncovered the scent of damp earth and putrid breath. She wrinkled her nose and turned her head, allowing her eyes to adjust to the darkness.

Her senses and the dim light of the moon revealed she lay on the ground next to the black dragon. A sound escaped her before she checked her reaction, and she fought to control the panic rising to the back of her throat. The dragon, who was her pillow, stirred slightly.

A shadow darker than the night closed over her as the dragon enveloped her with his leathery wing and tucked her closer. Only her head emerged from under its grasp. A lump of fear stuck in her throat kept her from screaming. It took long minutes before she realized the dragon slept.

Keep calm, carry on; keep calm, carry on, keep calm. . .

The mantra worked its magic and soothed her frazzled nerves. She swallowed the lump and breathed.

In control of herself once more, she opened one eye a hair's breadth. The moon passed its apex and headed towards dawn, and an army of stars twinkled in the night sky. Was she being watched? She closed her one peeking eye and listened for Hafnar. Deafening silence played in her ears.

Feeling braver, she turned her head and looked about, praying the beast wouldn't notice. Who knew how a dragon would react to being awakened unexpectedly? The thought of being a marshmallow roasted by dragon breath crossed her mind.

More alert than she had been in hours, she reached for Lachlan. The connection was instant, and he was with her.

"Lachlan, I don't have any idea where I am. The dragon is here with me but I can't tell if Hafnar is near or not. He's been drugging me. I suspect he thinks he's knocked me out for the night. But I dare not move. All I can see is the stars."

"Brenna, show me the stars ye see. Look straight up in the sky, directly above ye and show me."

Brenna knew little of astronomy. The hot tub in her backyard allowed for a certain amount of star gazing, and she enjoyed it, but her ability to identify anything beyond the most basic constellations was questionable. The North Star, the Big Dipper, and the Little Dipper were about all she could manage.

It was incredible when you really looked. No glowing city lights to dull the impact. The Highland sky, vast and beautiful.

Brenna focused her eyes on the heavens. The shape of a poorly made letter "H" separated itself from the millions of other stars.

Lachlan gazed into the night sky. "Lupus. The Wolfe. That is what ye see."

His sudden shift nearly caused him to tumble backwards, but quick maneuvering by Soren kept him seated. A blast of air blew from Soren's nostrils and he descended in tight circles touching down.

Once on solid ground Lachlan searched in earnest for the constellation seen through Brenna's eyes.

"There," he pointed in a northwesterly direction, and Soren turned to look. "Lupus is there." His skin crawled and his breath caught.

"I know where ye are. Ye're back on the Isle where ye rescued me."

Lachlan closed his eyes for a moment, and a heavy sigh escaped him. It made perfect sense that his brother would force him back to the cavern where he'd been prisoner for centuries. "Try and get some rest, Brenna. Soren and I will be doing the same. We'll be off before dawn and catch up within a few hours. Perhaps if yer feeling witty, you might stall a bit."

"Stall? You mean you want me to throw a hissy fit?"

"Aye. Anything ye can do to delay yer start on the morrow will help us catch up to ye."

"Ok. One super-sized hissy fit, coming up."

###

Lachlan felt the connection sever. He glanced at the sky just to make sure he had assumed her position correctly.

Soren stood wearily next to Lachlan. They had flown since morning, and lines of exhaustion etched Soren's face. He stood on two legs now, having shifted to his human form. He swayed as if a horrid wind threatened to topple him. Except the air was still this night.

"Shall we continue on, Lachlan?"

"No. We are close and must rest if we expect to have the strength to confront Hafnar and his dragon friend."

"Colin will never catch up to us by morning, even on Enbarr. Do we wait for him?" Soren asked.

"No. We can't afford to wait. The risk to Brenna is too great. It was the two of us held prisoner in the cavern. It will be the two of us who determine his fate."

"And what of Brenna's request to turn him over to the Fae court?" Soren asked.

"I hope she'll forgive us," he said, loosening the breastplate and stabbing the Answerer into the ground.

Fumbling for the Seer stone in the pouch at his waist, he withdrew the innocuous looking rock and rolled it between his fingers. He cupped his hand and brought the stone to rest in his palm, focusing his thoughts and remaining energy to its center.

The stone glowed from within and a spectrum of color radiated from the stone. Then the rainbow vanished and Ariel appeared.

"Lachlan. What news?"

"We've not exactly found them yet, but Brenna was able to reach me. They're on the Isle of Skye and are resting there until first light. The dragon is with her, but she could find no sign of Hafnar," Lachlan said.

"No doubt he stepped through a portal on Skye to return here to Faerie. Not likely he'd spend the night on the cold hard ground. He's probably snug in a warm bed somewhere in this realm. I wonder how many portals he's managed to open.

"I know the portal he must use to return to Skye. If I get there before he crosses, I can stop him. That would leave you only the dragon to contend with," Ariel said.

Lachlan nodded in approval. "We need to rest. We've only now just halted our search. Soren's stamina is admirable, but his foe is sleeping soundly, gathering strength. We'll set out in the hours before dawn," Lachlan said.

Ariel dropped the stone drop to her chest, severing the magic. Lachlan returned his to the pouch and hunkered down using one side of Soren's saddle as a pillow. Soren was already using the other side.

###

Ariel rose from her bed with purpose and dressed. She wrapped herself in one of Lachlan's old plaids. She had chosen sides and wanted Hafnar to know exactly which brother she chose to support. There would be no misunderstanding. She threw aside the heavy drape covering her window and craned her neck to see if the flag of her royal house flew atop the tower. Thank Danu, it did. Her father had returned home during the night.

"Are you coming with me, Tessa?"

The faerie dragon emerged from the bedcovers and yawned, spewing a stream of sparks over the edge of the bed and onto the floor. She rolled over to her back and displayed a complete lack of enthusiasm at the prospect of having to get up.

"Come on, lazy girl," Ariel said, scooping Tessa from the bed and onto her shoulder. The serpentine tail wound itself around her neck, and Tessa slumped, rather than perched on Ariel's shoulder.

Traipsing the labyrinth of castle hallways to her father's chamber took her through passageways she hadn't roamed in years. As a child she'd been innocent and naïve and absolutely sure her parents shared the proverbial faerie tale romance. The news had devastated her when she learned they didn't. Theirs had been an arranged marriage. Eventually, they had accepted one another, but her father's heart belonged to Lachlan's mother. Ariel had vowed to herself she'd never settle for a partner who was anything less than her own true love; and it was taking damn long for her to find him.

Ariel knocked on her father's door, and Tessa hissed as the sound echoed in the corridor. "Father, I must speak with you. I have news. Important news we must discuss."

Silence greeted her on the other side of the egress, solid oak and four inches thick. Then the door swung open, and her father appeared.

"Come in, Mouse." Her father stepped aside and bade her enter. He led her to the small leather couch by the fireplace. "Sit." He patted the seat next to him.

She plunked down on the sofa and took both her father's hands in her own. "Father, Lachlan is alive."

The color drained from his cheeks, and his mouth worked as if to speak, "I don't understand..."

Ariel gripped her father's hands more tightly. "He's alive, Father."

"But how?"

"He's been held captive all this time."

"You've seen him?"

"Yes. He is well."

Her father said nothing for a moment. "We gave up looking for him too soon." Regret. It slid from the corner of one eye and traveled a lonely path down the king's cheek. It dropped to his chest, where she knew he would feel the weight of it for eternity. "You're sure he is well?"

"I'm sure, Father."

The king stood. "I must see him for myself."

"Father, there is more you would know."

She told her father the tale of Lachlan's captivity; of Brenna, who risked her life for a stranger, and was now in need of rescuing herself; of Hafnar, who had been Lachlan's captor and keeper and who threatened them both.

"Hafnar has found a way to unseal at least one portal. I think I know which one. Lachlan needs our help. Will you help us?" she asked with quiet expectation.

Long moments passed. Finally, he pulled Ariel into a fierce embrace. "How long have you known, Mouse? Why did you not tell me sooner?"

"I wanted to tell you in person. This was not news I wanted passed to you by a royal messenger."

"How is it one of my children harbors such hatred for the other?"

"Help us find Brenna, Father."

"I'll send my most competent men to search for her and for Hafnar. I'll send word to the royal houses. If Hafnar is in our realm, he will be brought to me," he said in a cold, dead tone Ariel had never heard in her father's voice.

"Thank you, Father. Leave instructions for your men, then I'll meet you in the stables." Ariel pulled away from her father's arms, hurried from the room, and made for the barn. The king was not long behind.

The ride to the faerie gate that was passage to the Isle of Skye took only half an hour to reach. Ariel dismounted and left her mare in a stand of trees a few hundred yards from the portal and took up a post near a tall oak. The wide girth of its trunk hid her from view.

Her father remained closer to the gateway near an outcropping of stones. The dark mass of shadows cast by the rocks allowed him to blend into the background.

They waited.

CHAPTER SIXTEEN

Brenna tried to rest after she and Lachlan had agreed on a course of action, but her nerves prevented such a luxury. Truthfully, she worried more for Lachlan than for herself. Years of being held against his will would culminate in a reaction she could only guess at when he encountered his captor again.

The thought prompted the flow of her creative juices. She was smart; she could figure a way out of this predicament without having to involve Lachlan. She just had to think and get the hell out of here.

The dragon pillow slumbered soundly enough to keep the dead awake with its snoring, another reason she hadn't slept. Unsure how far she'd get if she tried to sneak off, she moved a bit under the leathery wing to gain a better look around. The first faint light of dawn brightened the horizon enough to determine they lay near a grouping of standing stones.

Stretching her neck and wishing for her chiropractor, she saw no sign of Hafnar. He had left the dragon to guard her and assumed the awful concoction he had given her would keep her knocked out.

She was at a complete loss as to what to do. In the end, she hoped the dragon slept soundly enough for her to sneak away and not get caught. Sometimes, simple was best.

The dragon snored, a rhythmic beat. He was certainly relaxed. He'd been more vigilant during the night, stirring each time she changed position on the stony hard ground. Hafnar had not called him by name, at least not that she had heard during her bouts of semi-consciousness. She wondered if he were a willing participant in her abduction or just another pawn following princely orders.

Sliding imperceptibly, she inched off her dragon pillow and lay prone on the grass. Creeping towards the portion of the dragon's wing strewn across the ground, she tentatively wrapped her fingers around the leathery tissue and lifted the wing, bit by agonizing bit. The wing was heavier than she expected and she remembered the daily swordplay Colin insisted on and sent a silent *thank you* to the man for playing the part of drill sergeant.

Once the wing lifted enough, she squiggled underneath and out from under the embrace of the creature and settled the wing back to the earth. She rolled to her belly for another look around.

Time was running out. The quickening of her pulse and a prickle at her nape warned her danger approached, or were her frazzled nerves about to give way under the pressure of the past few days?

She wanted nothing more than to be in Lachlan's arms. A piece of her was missing when separated from him. She lost her focus and shook her head to rid him from her mind. Still somewhat befuddled by Hafnar's concoction, she took a moment to gather her wits.

The sun began to rise above the horizon. Afraid her keeper would awaken when the sun's rays touched him, she crawled on all fours out of his line of sight.

She stood and ran with all the speed she could muster and bolted. Lord only knew how far she'd get, but it wouldn't be here with the dragon keeper, and that would be an improvement in her circumstance.

She hit top speed, but collided with something and flew backward onto her ass.

"Were you thinking to leave me, love?" Hafnar asked, glaring down at her.

"Shit! You are such an asshole." Her nerves snapped, her eyes filled, and twin tears of anger streaked down her cheek.

"We're almost there, my Brenna. Just a little longer, and you'll know exactly what I have planned for you. I'll give you a hint if you like. It's cold and dark and wet," he said.

Hafnar offered a hand to help Brenna up from the ground. She refused his assistance. Once on her feet, she brushed away the dirt from her clothing.

Hafnar moved suddenly, and before she could react, he had his arm wrapped around her neck and forced more of his potion down her throat. Brenna struggled and thrashed like a demon woman, biting his hand before the effects of the drug rendered her useless. She fell against Hafnar's chest.

"That's my good girl, Brenna. Now we can be off on our little adventure. You're going to be so surprised when we get there."

She passed out.

###

Ariel and King Ratava stood watch until the first rays of sun pierced the horizon. Salmon tendrils stretched across the sky revealing the dawn. Without exception, each sunrise in Faerie was vivid, picturesque, and perfect.

Now that the sun had cleared the horizon, it was evident they'd misjudged Hafnar's plan. She approached the stone behind which her father stood.

He stepped forward to meet her and said, "We'll need to come up with a new plan, Ariel."

"I'm glad you're here to help, Father. There is no telling how Hafnar will react once he learns you know of the crimes he's committed against Lachlan. He will not be pleased you show support for his enemy," she said.

"Lachlan is not Hafnar's enemy, he never was. Ruling this realm was never Lachlan's wish. All he wanted was to live a normal life. A mortal life. I can make that possible for him, and I will give him that, if he will allow it."

"Father, I must tell you, once this ordeal is over, I'd like to spend time with Lachlan in his world," she said with some trepidation, wondering about her father's reaction to her news.

He reached out to touch her arm, let his hand slide down its length and clasped her hand. He brought it gently to his mouth and kissed the back of her fingers. "I understand your decision. I don't think you'll change your mind on this point. It will be good for you to spend time amongst mortals. When you decide to come home, there will be a place for you here. I understand the desire you feel. It called me centuries ago, and I found Lachlan's mother in the mortal realm. Those were the happiest days of my life." He smiled at her and kept hold of her hand.

Ariel lifted the Seer stone from where it hung between her breasts and held it in her palm. She focused her attention and thoughts and the stone roared to life, carrying her voice to Lachlan.

"He didn't pass through this portal, Lachlan. I suspect he was never here to begin with," Ariel said.

"It's all right, lass. We're in the air, headed in Brenna's direction. I've not heard from her since last night. I told her to delay him if she could. He's giving her something to knock her out so she can't reach me. He must be back with her by now. If the portal is open, work your way to the west side of the island. Wait for my instructions."

"We're on our way, Lachlan." The tiny stone went black and the images vanished. "Come, Father, Lachlan has given me his directives." Alarmed at the thought of going on alone, she halted. "You are coming with me, aren't you?"

"Of course I am." He smiled at her.

Her father held her hand as they walked to the stand of trees where their mounts grazed. Ariel took a moment to absorb warmth from the sun and fortify herself for the task ahead. They mounted and cantered through the portal, and Ariel set a fast pace in a westerly direction. She wanted to be there when Brenna was found and to watch Hafnar's face when their father witnessed his treachery first hand.

###

Brenna couldn't rouse herself from whatever spell Hafnar had her under. He would have to kill her before he forced any more vile liquid down her throat. She reached for Lachlan, but couldn't muster the strength to maintain their connection. She struggled to open her eyes a crack, but her eyelids were so heavy they were impossible to lift. *Where am I*?

Leaden limbs refused to respond to her commands. Her arms and legs felt constrained somehow. The only thing she knew for sure was that she stood on the ground and was not seated upon the back of a dragon. They'd arrived, then, at whatever destination Hafnar had in mind for her.

The ordeal would be over soon. One way or another, whether Lachlan found her or not, it would be over. She recognized her defeated attitude. Admitted to herself the possibility that Hafnar would succeed in punishing Lachlan. In punishing her.

So much in life was a choice. She would fight to the end, however she could, with every ounce of strength she could muster. She would never surrender.

"Hafnar, you bastard! You will not defeat us! You will not defeat us! Do you hear me?" she shouted and her voice echoed in her bones.

The effort dispelled the cobwebs from her semi-conscious mind. Realization came swiftly. Arms and legs manacled and chained to the cavern wall. The icy waters of the Atlantic crept above her thighs. Torches shed their amber glow on either side of her and death approached one wave at a time.

Struggling against her bindings proved useless. Lachlan had battled them for centuries and hadn't escaped.

"Lachlan. The *cavern*. He's brought me to the cavern. The tide is rising."

And in her mind came his heartening response. "I'm almost there, lass."

###

The ocean consumed the tiny strip of rocky shore and left Soren nowhere to land. He stilled his wings, slowed his flight, and glided mere feet above the frigid North Sea.

Lachlan slid from the saddle and dropped into the icy waters a short distance from the opening to the cavern. The Answerer secured across his back, he fought against slamming into the side of the cliff.

A powerful wave threw him the last few feet into the mountain side. A jagged rock ripped open his sleeve and sliced the flesh of his shoulder. Blood ran, warm and thick from the wound. He ignored the pain and thanked Danu the fury of the waves hadn't cracked open his head.

He held to the cliff and waited for the next wave to push him through the narrow entrance of the cavern. Each incoming wave propelled him forward, and he fought to swim forward when the outgoing waves tried to suck him back out to sea.

Adrenaline pumped through his body and kept his mind clear and focused. Finally, he could stand with the water at his chest. He redoubled his efforts to reach Brenna, who stood a foot shorter than he. Time washed away with each wave.

"Brenna," he called out, desperate for her to hear him.

He reached the center of the cavern. Soren's prison. The water rose higher and keeping a foothold without losing ground became impossible. Forced to follow the outer curve of the cavern wall, he gripped the rocks and inched forward.

Time stopped as he struggled to reach her. Heavy breaths heaved from his chest and drowned all other sound save the pounding of his heart.

The darkness receded and shadows emerged, cast by burning torches.

"Brenna!"

The cavern curved around to the right. He planted his booted feet on the side of the cavern and waited for the next rush of a wave. He pushed with every ounce of strength and let the momentum of the wave carry him the last few yards around the bend.

Brenna struggled to keep above the water. The incoming waves washed over her head, allowing time for a single breath, timed to coincide with the trough of the outgoing wave.

She coughed and sputtered to clear a lung full of ocean water. One final reach and he clasped her arm in his grasp. He drew the Answerer from its scabbard with his free hand and sliced through a length of chain.

The water consumed her. There were no more troughs through which to breathe. The Answerer freed her other arm and Lachlan dove below the water searching for the manacles binding her ankles. He sliced the chains and pushed her to the surface.

A moment later he turned her back to his chest and wound his arms about her waist. He braced his feet against the wall of the cavern to keep them from smashing against it from the force of the pounding sea. Waves broke against his back and shoulders and sheltered her from the torrent giving her time to clear her lungs. They had to swim now to keep their heads above the water.

A glance at his shoulder confirmed he still bled, though it had slowed. Brenna shook violently in his arms. No words passed between them. He kissed her temple and she buried her face in the soft hollow of his neck. He held her and, with a little faerie magic, warmed her to stave off hypothermia.

"I'm going to turn around, lass, and ye'll need to be putting yer arms around my neck and we're going to swim out of here, understand?"

Brenna nodded.

He winced, and a muffled cry escaped him as her elbow gouged his battered shoulder. "Och, lass, mind the left shoulder. I've a bit of an injury." It worried him the wound hadn't healed in the time it took to free her.

"Oh, God, Lachlan, you're bleeding." She held on to him with one arm and applied pressure to the wound with the other. His muscles stiffened at her touch, but he remained stoic.

Waves beat them back and yet, Lachlan pulled them toward the entrance of the cave with each long, strong, stroke of his arms, and a little magical help she thought. Brenna fought to breathe as each wave broke over her. After several mouthfuls of salt water she learned to time her breath with Lachlan's strokes. It seemed an eternity had passed by the time they emerged from the cavern.

Soren circled the area and splashed down next to them. Lachlan clambered into the saddle. Brenna climbed on behind him and pried his fingers from the hilt of his sword. She sheathed Answerer in the scabbard across his back.

"He's injured himself, Soren.

"Yer fussing overmuch, lass. I'm fine."

One flap of his leather wings, and Soren lifted from the ocean and flew low along the water's edge, just high enough for his wings to clear the sea. He followed the shoreline until the ocean gradually rose in equal measure to the descent of a distant cliff.

The landing jarred Lachlan's teeth, and he bit his tongue. "Bloody hell, Soren. Are ye trying to kill me?"

Brenna slid from the dragon's back. Lachlan tried to muster enough grace to dismount and remain upright, but landed unceremoniously into a heap at Soren's feet.

Soren shimmered and transformed from dragon scales to human flesh. "You're a bloody mess, Brenna. Is that all Lachlan's blood or yours as well?"

"His. The blood is all his, but it's slowing now." She pushed Lachlan prone to the ground, tore his shirtsleeve, and wrapped the wound, knotting the ends in place. Then she straddled his arm and added her weight to his wounded shoulder to staunch the ooze of blood once and for all.

"Give me the Seer stone," Soren demanded of Lachlan, "I'll contact your sister." Once he held the stone in his hand, Soren focused his attention on the rock. He grunted in apparent frustration and flared his nostrils.

"Calm yourself, Soren. The stone isn't going to work if yer harried or frazzled," Lachlan said.

"Being hairy can't have ought to do with it. Ye've more hair than I, and you manage just fine."

The corner of Lachlan's mouth twitched slightly despite his current circumstance, but he didn't try to explain and simply allowed Soren to focus on his task.

Lachlan slid his free hand up Brenna's arm to the back of her neck and drew her closer. Dried salt tainted her lips.

"Thank Danu I found you in time."

Soren muttered a curse and a few wisps of smoke escaped his nostrils, but at last he seemed to be having some success with the stone. He knelt next to Lachlan as Ariel's image appeared so she could see him. Her black hair was unbound and flowing over her shoulders as she rode hard across a highland meadow. Lachlan noticed another puff of smoke curled lazily upward before it caught on a breeze and disappeared.

A smile crossed his face at this discovery. Soren blew smoke in anger, but also in desire. Dragons were fascinating creatures, indeed.

"Brenna, ye weigh as much as a fat Highland deer. Might ye get off my arm?" Lachlan asked.

"Did you just call me fat?"

"Aye."

Brenna contemplated his words, and when she didn't budge, Lachlan raised his forearm and grabbed her hip, pulling her off balance enough to remove his arm from between her legs. His Faerie blood was healing him, but too slowly by far. "On another occasion I'd be happy to put my arm between yer lovely thighs, but not just now, aye?"

A smile broke her lips in earnest. "I'll take that as a promise."

"Soren's saddle bags, lass. Two plaids are stowed within. Bring me one will ye?"

Brenna turned and hastened to his request. She returned to wrap the cloth around his shoulders.

"Yer shivering yerself. Ye'd best strip yer clothes and wrap yerself in the other one."

She returned to the saddle bag and drew out the remaining length of cloth. She glanced back at him and shrugged her shoulders. She'd no idea whatsoever to do with the plaid.

“Shall I ask Soren to assist me with this contraption?” she asked, sounding innocent.

He laughed when he realized she jested with him. “Nay, no one shall attend ye but I, understood?”

She winked at him and stepped behind an outcropping of boulders to change.

Lachlan shifted himself to a sitting position and returned his attention to the Seer stone. He regarded his sister for only a moment. She’d drawn her mount to a halt and waited for word from him. The sight of the man at her side chased away all thought and captured his rapt attention. His father.

“My son. Is it really you? I never thought I’d see you again.”

The time and distance between them faded to a heartbeat. Lachlan choked on the words he longed to say and stood frozen, staring into the Seer stone. Memories, lost through the centuries, flooded his mind and he fought to get a grip on the wave of emotions assailing him.

“Son, you’re injured.” Lachlan focused on his father’s words.

“It's but a scratch. Brenna bandaged it for me.”

Ariel frowned and pursed her lips. “Is there anything else amiss? Any other pain you neglected to mention in order not to worry her? You have a habit of downplaying your injuries.”

“There is no other injury, I swear it. I’d not mislead ye on what ails me, Mouse,” he said.

“Where is Brenna? Is she safe?” Ariel asked.

“She’s well. Tired and still feeling the effects of Hafnar’s poison, but she is alive and safe.” His heart swelled with unspoken emotion.

“Let us gather at the standing stones on Skye. You and father can shift us back to Colin’s B&B. Then we’ll discuss how to deal with Hafnar,” Lachlan said.

“Agreed. But first we celebrate.” Ratava’s smile mirrored Lachlan’s.

The Seer stone blinked out, assuming its role as an ordinary rock. Lachlan closed his hand and raised his fist to the center of his chest where his heart lay.

CHAPTER SEVENTEEN

Excitement thrummed through Lachlan at seeing his father. He'd missed him nearly as much as Ariel. The king himself taught him to use the powers inherited from his Fae ancestry. Early on in his lessons, he'd set the highland spring grasses aflame, brought a loch to boil, and turned his father's favorite falcon into a toad. Still, the training continued and, eventually, his skills improved, his father ever patient. He'd lost most of his abilities during his imprisonment.

Brenna emerged from the outcropping of stones, his plaid draped around her like a Roman toga. "Are ye ready to meet my father, lass?"

"I'm not exactly dressed for the occasion, but I guess I'll have to do."

"My father will only see the woman who saved his son." He stepped forward and squeezed her shoulders. "I was terrified I'd lost ye to the sea. Tell me ye changed yer mind about turning Hafnar over to the Fae court, now that he's nearly taken yer life, because, I'm no' sure I can keep from killing the bastard."

Brenna leaned into his chest, and he embraced her. Dried salt crystals dusted the skin of her shoulders and back, a reminder of how close he'd come to losing the woman he loved.

"No. You must turn him over. I'm a psychologist. He can be rehabilitated with the proper treatment. That can't happen if he's dead."

Lachlan sighed. "Bloody hell, lass. Ye'd give a wolf a second chance in a flock of sheep wouldn't ye? I can't give ye my word on this, Brenna. Ye should know that."

Brenna looked up at him. Her storm colored eyes searched his, and her lips tilted upward in a half smile. "You'll do the right thing, when the time comes."

Soren grunted at her words. "Let's ride," he said and shifted to his beastly form.

The dragon snorted, wisps of smoke ringing the air. Lachlan understood the dragon's ill temper. They both wanted Hafnar dead. Lachlan helped Brenna up onto Soren's back and he settled in behind her. "It's all right, my friend."

Soren sprang to the air and took command of the wind. The air raced past them, chilling her, and she quivered with cold. He wrapped her in the safety of his arms and lent her his warmth. He wanted her. Home. In his bed. Where he could warm her properly.

They arrived first at the stand of stones marking the portal, but the wait for Ariel and his father was brief. Ariel slowed her mare and dismounted, running to Lachlan, a wide smile splitting her face. Tessa flapped her gossamer wings and rose from Ariel's shoulder. The faerie dragon proceeded directly to Soren and settled between the thorny protrusions of his crest.

Ariel embraced her brother and squealed in that way women sometimes do, when words cannot convey the joy in their hearts.

Lachlan approached his father, who'd reined in next to Ariel and alighted from his horse. A man forever in his prime. The years hadn't grizzled his hair, or etched his face, or dulled his eyes. Ratava eyed Lachlan down and up. Was he evaluating what time and captivity had taken from his son?

The king squared his shoulders and bridged the distance between them. He opened wide his arms and hugged his son. A strong, overpowering hug that he held for long moments.

"I never should have stopped looking for you, Son. Can you ever forgive me?" He pulled away reluctantly and waited for Lachlan's answer.

"I'm here now. A free man. Once Hafnar is captured and punished, my life will begin anew. I couldn't ask for more than that."

The king turned to Brenna and lifted her hand. He placed a kiss upon her knuckles. Pink flushed her skin and her gaze dropped to her feet.

"It is an honor to meet you, Brenna. I owe you a debt of gratitude for giving me back my son."

"The honor is mine Your Majesty." Brenna bowed slightly.

"You did what a full blooded Fae king could not. You found my son and brought him back to us."

"Ariel, take Soren and Brenna back the B&B. I'd like a moment with my father, if ye don't mind."

###

Brenna burst through the front door of the B&B, leaving Ariel and Soren to traipse in after her. She checked the tapestry on the wall and exhaled a sigh of relief. She still existed within its weave. Satisfied, she bounded up the tower stairs, two at a time, heading for the room she and Lachlan shared. She had never been more embarrassed in her life. Meeting a Fae king wrapped in nothing but a tartan. It wasn't so much his status as king, but rather his status as Lachlan's father that caused her to fret. Oh well, she'd endured more embarrassing moments. Truthfully, he'd been quite kind, and more than anything, thankful.

Brenna showered to wash the ocean off her and remove any traces of Hafnar's touch. She ran a brush through her hair, then rummaged through her suitcase at the end of the bed and pulled out a pair of her jeans. She did the squiggle dance to get them over her hips, then threw on a knitted wool sweater and pulled on her Durango boots. The frigid Atlantic still chilled her blood. She'd faced death and it wasn't pretty.

Her life. She had nearly lost her very life in that cavern. The shock of her near death experience overwhelmed her senses. Her hands shook as she tried to fold the discarded plaid into some semblance of neatness. Her bottom lip quivered and she bit down hard to keep to stay its trembling. It didn't work.

Tears pooled and spilled over the rim of her lower eyelids. Rivulets washed down her face and great gasps of breath caught in her throat, choking her.

"Brenna, are you all right?" Ariel asked from the doorway.

Brenna drew in a ragged breath. "Of course. Everything is fine."

Ariel pushed the door wider and let herself in. "I know we've only just met, but you don't look fine."

Brenna sniffled. "Just once in my life, I'd like to do the right thing and have everything work out, but it never happens that way. Someone always got the shaft in the end, and it's usually me. Oh, God listen to me. I'm whining. I'm just exhausted." She sighed and scrubbed her face. "I care so very much for your brother. But he's immortal. I'm not. That will make for a difficult relationship."

"Maybe it's not as bad as it seems," Ariel said.

"What? Well, right now, it feels like a nightmare."

"My brother is half mortal. There was a time when a gash such as the one on his shoulder would have healed without the use of a needle to stitch it up. No other Fae has endured what he has for as long as he did. He's died countless deaths while captive in that cave. At the end, he was on the verge of losing his immortality. He may lose it yet. Don't give up hope, Brenna. No one yet knows how the story will end."

Ariel sat on the bed and motioned for Brenna to sit beside her. Long minutes passed and neither of them moved, cocooned in the silence. "He loves you. I can see it plainly on his face when looks at you. I know him. There's nothing he won't do for you, so just love him and forget the rest. He'll find a way."

Tessa flitted into the room, tittering loudly and circling above them.

"Come on, let's go downstairs and get you something to eat."

Brenna rolled up her sleeves and headed to the bathroom to splash water on her face, washing away the salt from her tears. "I think I need a drink."

Tessa preceded them down the stairs, squeaking and sputtering along the way. She glided directly to Soren when they entered the great hall, obviously enamored with the man dragon. Brenna put on her happy face and met Lachlan's intense green gaze from across the room. Colin was with them. He must have hitched a ride on the faerie bus. The men had seated themselves at the great hall table, tankards of ale at their places. Lachlan looked exhausted. Stress lines creased the corners of his eyes when he smiled at her, relief apparent in his audible sigh. Her heart swelled with emotion when he reached out a hand to her. King Ratava lifted an eyebrow as he took in her jeans and cowboy boots, but smiled in acceptance nonetheless. Brownie points for the king.

Ariel went directly to her brother and stood behind him, examining the damage to his shoulder.

"How is the pain?" she asked.

"It's naught but a scratch really. I hardly notice it."

Ariel raised her eyebrow and made an indistinct noise in the back of her throat that seemed to indicate she thought he was being somewhat less than truthful. Ariel tended the wound by removing the knotted remnant of the linen shirt Brenna had used as a bandage. "I'm going to need to stitch your cut. It's deep enough to stitch, but not severe enough to warrant magic."

Colin produced a first aid kit and Ariel cleaned and disinfected the wound, then set to work with a needle and thread.

"I don't understand why ye fuss so over these things. It's not like I'm going die from these scratches. If centuries of drowning in a cavern didn't do it, I can't think a wee wound such as this would do me in."

"In case you haven't noticed, you are healing more slowly these days brother." Ariel exchanged a knowing look with Brenna. "Perhaps you are more mortal than you think?"

The comment seemed to set him back, and he frowned at her. "Aye, what do ye make of that?"

"What I make of it is that you are half mortal and maybe with that will eventually come mortality," she replied.

Brenna turned to King Ratava. "Is it true? Do you think he'll eventually turn mortal?"

The king thought for long moments, his gaze never wavered from hers. He shook his head. "No. If there is Fae blood in his veins, he will retain his immortality."

Ariel didn't spout back to defend her point. She merely accepted the king's answer and continued to stitch her brother's wound.

Lachlan ran a hand through his hair and sighed. It didn't seem to be the answer he wanted to hear.

Brenna's moment of hope at Ariel's words squashed. What she wanted could never happen, and the sooner she accepted it and moved on, the better off they'd both be. She bit her lip, keeping the tears at bay.

"We need all our heads together to plan our next attack. I'll not wait idly for Hafnar to catch us off guard. Brenna is not to be alone for even a moment. One of us must be with her at all times. Are we clear?"

Everyone nodded in the affirmative. Brenna's blood pressure ticked up a notch. She'd been taking care of herself for years, yet here, she needed protection and that irked. She could feel the king's gaze on her. Watching, surmising, and pushing at the edge of her thoughts.

True to Lachlan's edict, over the next days, Brenna relinquished her privacy. Ariel comforted her with her presence and distracted her from the ache in her heart.

Either Colin or Soren was always on guard. And the nights. The nights she spent snuggled in Lachlan's arms, wishing the sun would forget to rise.

###

Brenna nestled in the crook of his arm, her pearl white skin radiant as the first light of dawn. A cacophony of iron swords clanked and arrows whooshed and whistled through the air. The men prepared themselves for battle with Hafnar. Loath to wake her from slumber, Lachlan eased his arm out from under her.

Eyelashes fluttered and gray eyes cracked open to peek at the new day. Brenna stretched languorously and wrapped her arms around Lachlan's neck pulling him to her lips for a morning greeting.

"How much time do we have left?" she asked.

"Not much. We leave today to begin searching for Hafnar."

Her brows drew together, and her forehead furrowed. "Well then. We'd better get moving. I'm sore and starving after last night." She winked at him remembering their passion filled night and slipped out from beneath him to dress.

They arrived together in the hall as Ariel set out trays laden with food she'd conjured out of thin air. The men filed in one by one and took a seat at the table. They passed the platters and heaped food upon their plates, clearly famished after their morning practice.

Lachlan filled a plate and sat at the table. Brenna helped herself to a cup of steaming coffee and a dish of bacon and eggs.

"What news have we of Hafnar?" asked Lachlan.

King Ratava cleared his throat. "Trinket arrived this morning bearing news. Hafnar has been detained in

Faerie." The king turned to Brenna and explained, "Trinket is a Sylph. She has served as my messenger for over a millennium."

Lachlan scrubbed his face with his hands and leaned forward in his chair. "Father, if ye could unseal the nearest portal, then ye and Ariel can see Soren and me through to Faerie. Colin, I entrust Brenna to your care while I am gone."

"Whoa, wait a minute." Brenna held out a hand. "I'm not disagreeing with your idea, Lachlan, but what makes you think I'll be staying behind with Colin?" Brenna turned to him. "No offense intended, Colin."

Colin's lips turned up at the corners. "None taken."

"I'll not have ye traipsing around in Faerie while Hafnar is there. My bastard brother—sorry, Father—would be happy to kill ye before my very eyes. Yer safer here.

"I disagree—"

"I'll not be discussing this any further, lass. Yer staying. Besides, mortals are forbidden in Faerie. Should the Dark Fae discover yer there, ye'd be in even more danger."

Ariel wrapped an arm around Brenna's shoulders, drew her close, and flashed her brother an angry look. Tessa spat a rain shower of sparks in his general direction, obviously choosing sides.

Brenna's eyes shot figurative sparks too. "But I'm not through—"

Lachlan shoved his chair back from the table. "Enough." He slammed his fist down. "Colin, Brenna is staying until I return. Under guard. I'm sorry, lass. I'll not risk yer safety again."

Brenna knocked her chair completely over in her rush to stand. Her jaw worked up and down, but no words formed, only an exasperated cry forced itself through her clenched teeth. She stalked from the room, hands fisted at her sides.

Lachlan righted her chair and plunked down, propping his elbows on the table and dropping his face into his hands. "That didn't go so well did it?"

"You were downright mean to her." Ariel stood with one hand on her hip, "I can't believe you would speak to her that way."

"This isn't the time for this discussion, Ariel."

Emerald eyes flashed fire at him, and Ariel stomped toward the main entry. "Let's move it, dragon."

Soren stood, patted Lachlan on the back and leaned close to whisper, "You're two for two, my friend."

"Bloody hell." He ran his hands through his hair. Lachlan glanced at his father. "Have you anything to say?"

"My boy, I would say after six hundred years, you are a little out of practice dealing with the fairer sex."

"Hrumpf. Do you not think she is safer here?" Lachlan asked.

"With Hafnar detained in Faerie, I don't see that she is in any more danger there than here. As for the Dark Fae, it will take time for them to discover her presence. But what matters is what you think, Son."

"Bloody hell." Lachlan pushed away from the table and made his way to the stairwell. Brenna sat on the top stair. She sniffled and stuck her nose in the air at sight of him.

"I thought you'd have left by now."

"With ye peeved at me?" He sat on the landing next to her. "I came to apologize. I fear for ye, lass. I would never forgive myself if something were to happen to you when I could have prevented it."

"Nothing will happen to me. You, Ariel, and your father are Fae, and Soren is a dragon for crying out loud. I would think I'd be safer with the four of you than staying here with Colin. I'm sure he's a powerful man, but I'd still rather go with you. And the cloak, I could wear the cloak and not even be seen while I'm there. Please, Lachlan. Reconsider."

She did make a point. There would be a whole army of Fae warriors to defend them in Faerie. Perhaps he hadn't thought it through quite enough.

"All right, lass."

A look of delight crossed her features and she smiled broadly. "Thank you, Lachlan. You won't regret it." She reached for his hand and pulled him down the stairwell behind her.

###

Colin stayed behind while the others mounted up and headed for the stones housing the nearest portal to Faerie. Colin couldn't convince Lachlan to let Brenna drive them to the passage. He insisted he would take Enbarr, and therefore the others would ride as well. She made a mental note she'd teach him to drive when they returned.

Lachlan and his father wore somber faces, and their expressions suggested they were unsettled at the prospect of facing Hafnar. Then there was Soren. Ribbons of smoke wafted from his nostrils with each breath, and Brenna wondered if he would suffer from smoke inhalation if his temper continued to simmer over finally confronting Hafnar.

They stepped within the circle of standing stones that housed the portal to Faerie. At first, the silence unnerved her. The large stones surrounded her, giving her the sense of being shut in. She glanced around and took comfort at the ease of stance in the others. And then she heard a soft whistling, barely audible, so soft she wasn't sure she heard anything. Within seconds it grew louder, becoming distinct and high pitched, undeniably inhuman. Brenna's world spun, and her bones vibrated within her body like a tuning fork. She shook uncontrollably, and a mind numbing cold stripped her of sensation. It was as though every appendage fell asleep even where there were no appendages. She grabbed onto Lachlan's arm. The stones screeched so loudly she feared her eardrums would rupture. She realized she was screaming along with them, adding to the dissonance.

A sickening sensation of falling from a great height overwhelmed her and the wall of sound pounded her from all sides. Sensation returned in the form of knife edged pain, slashing each cell in her body. The blood boiled in her veins and stopped her heart. She floated weightlessly on an ocean of air, directionless she drifted within the Faerie portal. Her body dissolved, each cell spiraling on its own course.

Snippets of Lachlan's voice drifted in and out of her subconscious, pulling her towards him. He stretched out an arm for her, but she was beyond his reach. Her cells drew closer and closer, and a vacuum of the ether slammed them together. The portal spewed her from its maw and pummeled her into the ground. She'd been hit by a truck—or something like a truck—she would swear it.

A wave of spots fell like rain across her line of sight. Hafnar's laughter echoed in her ears, and a sharp pain punched her face. The spots collided, formed a pool of darkness, and she blacked out. . .

CHAPTER EIGHTEEN

Unease settled in Lachlan's chest like a sickness. Columns of dark smoke rose from the ground near the portal and the air was thick with the bitter stench of spent magic. An ominous silence surrounded them. He glanced around. Brenna and his father hadn't crossed through the portal. Something had gone horribly wrong. Trinket's lifeless body lay in the grass just yards from Lachlan.

Kneeling down beside the lifeless sylph, he gently lifted her from her resting place and held her in the palm of his hand. Her throat had been slit. "Bloody hell. Who would do such a thing to a mere messenger? A royal messenger at that."

Ariel flashed him a look and shook her head.

The touch of Lachlan's half human hand set in motion the Fae laws of self-preservation that protected even the dead from discovery. A wisp of smoke rose from beneath her, then a tiny flame erupted consuming her body in seconds leaving nothing behind but a fistful of ashes.

Lachlan scattered them in the meadow.

"Where the hell are Brenna and Father?" Lachlan said.

Ariel looked about in horror. Her eyes grew wide and she put one foot forward, into the portal and leaned in to look. A moment later, she jumped back and away from the passage. "Oh, dear Danu, the portal. It's crumbling. It might be passable I can't be sure, but it looks bad."

He'd lost her.

"No." His voice boomed through the faerie meadow.

Lachlan reached for Brenna's mind. He found nothing but darkness, a hollow emptiness he couldn't define. He could sense her presence lurking, but somehow unresponsive. Powerless. Just as he'd been when he was chained to the cavern wall. Only now, he'd lost the ability to reach her.

Soren strode to the center of the circle and plucked something shiny from the ground, holding it up for Lachlan to see. "Is this familiar to ye?"

"Aye," Lachlan said, taking the object from Soren. "It's my father's coronation ring." He held it in his palm, testing the ring's weight. The emerald cut ruby stone twinkled in his hand, warm to the touch like a candle flame. He slipped it on his finger. Why? Why was his father's ring lying in the grass?

" Ye have to repair the portal, Mouse," Lachlan said.

Ariel's shoulders dropped with the weight of his words. "I don't know how." Tears spilled onto her cheeks, and she dropped her gaze.

Lachlan took her hand and kissed her knuckles. "Well then, we'll figure it out together. Come. We must find the captain of the guard and tell him about Trinket. Then we'll deal with our brother.

"If there's anything written about the magic required to repair the portal, my guess is we will find it with Father's journals." Ariel turned and ran toward the castle. The men followed on her heels. The castle floated a hundred feet above them, tethered by ropes. An explosion of color caught Lachlan's attention and pulled his eyes to the top of the tallest castle tower. A hot air balloon with a rainbow colored canopy descended like an apparition.

Ariel unlatched the woven door of the gondola and they stepped aboard.

Propelled by magic, the balloon lifted off and a light breeze assailed them with the scent of salt from the faerie sea. The craft slowed its ascent and hovered near the tallest tower. A drawbridge dropped and they disembarked. Despite his years absent, Lachlan knew the way. They passed freely through the maze of halls to King Ratava's library. Lachlan paused along the way to instruct a servant to send him Captain Regan.

"Father keeps his personal records up there." Ariel pointed to the topmost shelf of the massive mahogany bookshelf. She crooked her finger in a beckoning gesture, and the journals tumbled from their lair, stacking themselves neatly in her outstretched hands.

Each enormous volume encompassed centuries of thoughts, ideas, musings, and magic. Lachlan hesitated to peruse the stack of memories. It seemed a violation for the three of them to be poring through his father's intimate thoughts.

It didn't matter. Nothing mattered but getting to Brenna as quickly as possible. He sank into the buttery leather couch and cracked open the worn binding of one of the books. Ariel handed a tome to Soren, then sat on one side of the king's desk. Soren settled opposite her.

The king had separated his thoughts and categorized them: One volume for ideas and challenges related to running his portion of Faerie, one for daily chronicles, and one specific to magic. Lachlan focused on the magic section.

"Look at this." Ariel held a tome, larger than the rest. Lachlan rose and looked over her shoulder. The blood red leather binding rose and fell with the intricate embossment of their family crest. Runes edged the spine, and a wide elaborate silver clasp held it firmly shut to prying eyes.

Slender fingers fiddled with the latch, searching for a way to open the book. "I don't know how to open it," she said.

"Use your magic, Mouse."

She lifted a brow and glared at him. "I've tried that already." She stood and motioned for him to sit in her stead. "You try."

The moment Lachlan touched the book an arc of blue light sizzled across the silver bindings, and he yanked his hands away. He looked to Ariel, then to Soren, seeking acknowledgment they'd seen the arc of light as well.

Soren reached across the desk and rested a hand on the journals cover.

Nothing.

Soren pushed the book closer to Lachlan and said, "I think it recognizes ye."

"I've never seen it before. How can it know me?" Lachlan extended his hand, nearly touching the surface. The blue light arced again, from the clasp to the ring he wore on his forefinger.

"Your father's ring. It thinks ye're him," Soren said.

"He's right. The ring is the key." Ariel settled on the edge of the desk. "Do you suppose Father left the ring behind on purpose?"

Lachlan slipped the ring from his finger. The stone, neatly encased by a symmetrical filigree cross, mirrored the image of the silver clasp they sought to open. The cerulean light flashed, dancing over the ring and the clasp. Once he settled the ring into the cradle of the clasp, the light ceased and the latch fell open onto the desk.

"Lachlan, my old friend." Regan's face brightened as he entered the study. He offered a greeting and Lachlan clasped the man's forearm in response.

"'Tis good to see you, my man. Though the circumstances could be better. Tell me, where has Hafnar been detained?" Lachlan asked.

Regan quirked an eyebrow and shook his head. "My Lord, we search for him, but so far we've had no luck."

"Bloody hell." Lachlan turned to his companions. "The bastard set us up. He's not here. We're trapped on this side of the portal and Brenna's on the other." He ran a hand through his hair, fisted his hands, and bellowed a series of curses.

Ariel touched his arm to sooth him. "Sit. The answer is in here. It has to be." She pushed their father's book in front of him. Lachlan flipped through the pages and searched.

###

The sonic boom signaled something was horribly wrong. The sound struck Colin dumb. Moments passed before he ran from the kitchen to the great room to lay eyes upon the tapestry. Brenna was gone. Only Lachlan remained seated upon Enbarr, his countenance intent, eyebrows drawn together in a scowl.

Colin ran for the front door heading for the Porsche Cayenne. He gunned the vehicle, spitting gravel. Minutes passed like hours until at last Colin brought the vehicle to a stuttering stop.

There was no road leading directly to the stones, and he ran the last quarter mile. As he approached the spot, the hairs on his forearms rose and gooseflesh crept along his neck. An involuntary shiver swept through him.

Smoke and bits of flame erupted along a twenty-foot radius surrounding the portal. Brenna lay in the center of the circle of stones, face down, hair strewn over the ground in knotted disarray. He ran the last yards to her side, dropped to his knees, and reached his hand to the artery just below her jaw.

A strong, steady pulse.

Colin closed his eyes for a moment and gave thanks to whatever power had kept her alive. He touched her, checking for bodily damage.

Her left arm was broken, no doubt about it, given the impossible angle. He turned her onto her back, mindful of her injury, and discovered her face covered in blood. He pushed her blood soaked hair out of the way to find the source. Probably a broken nose, too. She must have arrived as he found her, face first.

She twisted and turned on the ground regaining consciousness. Struggling still, against whatever force spit her back into this realm.

"Brenna, can ye hear me? It's all right, stop yer struggles or ye'll hurt yerself more than ye have already."

"Colin?"

"Aye, Miss Sinclair, I'm here."

"Where are the others? Are they safe?"

"They must have made it through to Faerie. They're not here. We've got to get ye to the doctor. You've a broken arm, and yer nose took a mighty beating as well."

At the sound of his voice, she quieted and ceased her struggle, slipping back into the dark oblivion. He lifted her into his arms and carried her to the SUV. He gently eased her into the backseat.

Twenty minutes on the road put them in the center of town in front of the building that housed the only local clinic. Colin pounded on the door of the small infirmary. From an upstairs window an unkempt head poked out. "What is it?"

"I have a patient for ye, doc," Colin said.

"I'll be right down." A minute passed, and then the door opened. The doctor, hair as messy as when he had looked outside, let them in. He'd tucked his pajama top into a pair of trousers. "Bring her in here."

The clinic was well equipped to handle such emergencies as were typical to the working folk of the highlands. Her nose turned out to be badly bruised, not broken. She had a concussion and had broken her arm cleanly when she braced for her inelegant landing, saving her face so to speak. Dr. Morrison adeptly set Brenna's arm and gave her a generous dose of painkillers.

An hour later, patched up and eager to leave, Brenna hefted herself off the metal table. She stumbled into

Colin's arms. She didn't pay an ounce of attention to Dr. Morrison's instructions, but nodded dutifully.

As soon as the doctor left the room, Brenna looked up at Colin and mumbled, "Let's go. I have to get back to the stones."

"Ye can barely stand up on yer own, Miss Sinclair. We're going home for now," Colin said.

"But where are they? We have to see if they're okay." Brenna's words slurred.

"They've gone through to Faerie. Ye were the only one who didn't cross over. Now we're going home and ye'll rest."

She wanted to argue with the man, but her thoughts were muddled. The work of the painkillers, she surmised. Rest. Yes, she had to rest.

They left the clinic just as the sky exploded with rapid fire thunder and lightning bolts cleaved the sky. A chill swept up Colin's nape. Had the portal spit forth another?

Brenna paid no attention to the odd storm and said few words on the trip back to MacGregor B&B, only sniffled loudly like an inconsolable child.

The sound of gravel under the tires roused Brenna enough to sit up and take notice. Colin cut the engine. She jumped out and lost her balance to a spell of dizziness. Colin steadied her. He lifted her up and carried her up to the tower room she shared with Lachlan. He laid her gently on the mattress.

"Are they here, Colin? Did they come back?"

Colin shook his head.

"Why didn't Lachlan come back for me?"

"He has work to do in Faerie, Miss Sinclair. And while he is there, you will stay here and heal. I'll see to yerr safety until he returns. Now rest."

###

The first rays of sun flitted through the stained glass windows throwing shards of light throughout Brenna's chamber. Prying open an eye, she peeked about the room, then buried her head under her pillow and pulled the comforter over her head, incapable of facing the day. Physical and mental exhaustion wreaked havoc with her body and mind. Worry over the safety of the others safety kept her from falling back to sleep.

Every muscle in her body ached and screamed for her not to move. Her casted arm throbbed, and her head pounded from the concussion. And so it began, a pity party of epic proportions got underway less than twelve hours after being spewed from the portal to Faerie.

Colin hastened into the room carrying a tray.

"I'm not hungry." Her voice sounded like that of a petulant child, even to her own ears.

"I'll leave it here until ye are. And ye need to rest so ye'll be staying in that bed."

He placed the tray on the nightstand. It contained a sleeve of saltines, a bottle of painkillers, and a pitcher of water.

"Thanks for the care package. Though a fifth of whisky might have done just as well."

"I was saving that for after dinner."

"Any sign of them yet?" she asked.

"Not yet."

Brenna threw aside the comforter and swung her feet onto the floor. "I have to get to the stones. I have to see what's happened."

Colin grabbed her arm and steadied her. "Ye'll not be going anywhere, Miss Sinclair. Sit yer arse back down on that bed."

"But I—"

"Brenna. For whatever reason, the portal would not let you cross. The stones will tell ye nothing. Yer not Fae, so ye can't cross on yer own. There is nothing there to see except stones."

She stared at him a long moment as she considered his words.

"He will come back for me, Colin. He will." She squeezed her eyes shut to keep them from leaking tears. Lachlan would to return to her. As soon as he'd dealt with Hafnar, he'd be back.

His features softened. "Aye. I'm sure he will. Here, I want ye to wear this." He slipped a bracelet over her wrist. An enormous sapphire glittered in the center of the wide gold cuff, flanked all around by blue diamonds.

"Why do you want me to wear it?"

"It's an ancient Fae hallow, one that will afford ye protection against black magic and evil intent."

"But Hafnar is detained in Faerie. Why would I need this now?"

He scowled and raised a brow. "I thought women liked such baubles?"

"Well, that's a bit of a generalization, but I agree. Where did you get this?"

"I…am somewhat of a collector of…baubles. As luck would have it, this one just arrived today. I purchased it in an auction last week. Now rest." He left her to her misery. The man held his secrets close, and she was too tired to ponder over them. She choked down a painkiller and flattened a Saltine to the roof of her mouth, letting it turn to mush before she swallowed it. She buried her head under the pillow.

It seemed only minutes before the clickety-clack of high heels resonated in the hallway and nudged Brenna from her hibernation. The sound stopped outside her door and a faint recognition registered. Brenna dismissed it as a drug induced dream and curled in a fetal position. A muffled scratching ensued.

She pushed the pillow off her face. "Colin?"

The door opened a crack. Ray bans and ruby red lipstick peered in at her.

"Jen, is that you?"

A squeak of delight emanated from six inches off the ground, and Merlin bounded into the room.

"You look like hell, Bren."

Brenna cracked a smile, then bit her bottom lip to still its quivering. "I can't believe you're here."

Jen entered the room and clicked the door closed behind her. She swept Merlin off his feet and placed him on the bed with his mistress. He greeted Brenna with a gentle lick to her cheek and then disappeared beneath the comforter.

Jen perched on the edge of the bed. "Colin called me yesterday. He told me what happened and sent me a ticket on the first flight out.

"I don't imagine he gave you any choice in the matter, but I'm so glad you came."

"Don't you worry about anything besides getting better. I'll take care of you and we'll figure everything out."

"He's gone, Jen. I've lost him" Brenna pinched the bridge of her nose and sighed.

"The fat lady isn't singing yet, so don't you dare give up, you hear me? This whole Faerie portal collapsing thing will get fixed, and Lachlan will come back. Now, I'm going to get a bath running for you. You'll feel better once you're cleaned up. Then I'll fix you something to eat."

"I'd feel better if I were dead or drunk. I'm not sure which has greater appeal at the moment. Colin promised me whisky for dinner."

"That bad, huh?"

"I don't know which hurts worse, my heart, my head, or my arm." Brenna massaged her temple with the heel of her hand. "Oh God, that's worse."

The spots were back, clouding Brenna's vision, and this time they morphed to the size of basketballs. She closed her eyes and covered her face with her good arm.

"Ohhhh, where did you get this?" Jen lifted Brenna's arm away from her face and fondled the bracelet. She plucked it from Brenna's wrist to try it on.

"Colin. It's supposed to protect me."

Merlin crawled out from under the comforter and barked at Jen.

"One minute, you monster." Jen switched the bracelet to her other wrist and held it out to inspect it.

Dissatisfied with her response, Merlin planted his butt down and howled. Incessantly.

Jen clicked her tongue. "Fine. I need to feed your little heathen. I'll be back in five."

Brenna watched Merlin trot to the door with Jen on his heels. She had five more minutes to wallow in self-pity. She covered her face with the pillow, blocking out the light. The cool cotton of the pillowcase soothed her throbbing head for a moment before it warmed to her body temperature. If she'd been thinking properly, she'd have asked Jen for an ice pack. *There really should be an intercom in these rooms.*

She willed her body to relax and slowed her breathing, encouraging her body to melt into the mattress instead of tensing like a steel spring. The pillow stifled her breath and she reached to push it aside.

She couldn't move it.

The subtle weight of the feathers and down grew leaden. A shock of pain from the weight of the pillow pressing on her badly bruised nose shimmied through her skull. Her head pounded, and she gasped for a breath. Squirming and ripping at the pillowcase did nothing to allow even a shallow breath of air to enter her lungs.

Hafnar, you fucking bastard. I swear to God, I will kill you myself.

Brenna flailed about and managed to knock the pitcher of water from the nightstand onto the floor where it shattered. Someone pounded on her bedroom door.

A muffled scream pushed the last of the air from her lungs, and she slammed her fist on the nightstand. Blood flowed thick and warm from her nose; she feared she would drown in it.

"Brenna! Move yer hands away," Colin said, his voice urgent and demanding.

She ceased her thrashing, and Colin ripped the pillow to shreds. Feathers floated to the floor and as quickly as the incident began, it was over. No lead after all.

She wiped her face with the back of her hand and stared at the bloody mess. Colin rushed to the bathroom and brought her a wet towel.

"Hafnar hasn't been detained after all. What do we do now?"

"Downstairs. My office in ten minutes," Colin said and stormed from the room. "Miss Baker," Colin bellowed, "get her dressed and downstairs. Now. And put that bloody bracelet back on her. She's not to take it off again. Ever."

Jen skittered into the room. "Crap. I think he's pissed."

"You don't suppose he's going to kill me himself do you?" Brenna asked.

"Of course not, but he'll feel better if he gives you a lecture. What the hell bird exploded in here? Never mind, come on, I'll help you dress."

Ten minutes later, they stood outside Colin's office door. Brenna raised her hand and rapped on the door.

"Enter."

Brenna pushed open the office door. "Look Colin, I don't need another lecture about--oh, my God."

King Ratava stood and opened his arms wide, beckoning Brenna closer.

She stepped into his embrace. "The others? Where are they?"

CHAPTER NINETEEN

King Ratava tightened his embrace and squeezed the air from her lungs. "They have crossed to Faerie."

"But why aren't you with them?" Her brows drew together and her lips formed a stiff line that slashed her face.

"Hafnar's magic. I could sense it in the portal and I knew something was terribly wrong. Once I could see you weren't going to make it across to my realm, I tried to follow you. I got tossed out in the year 2080 and it took a bit of finagling to find my way back to you. The portal is collapsing. All of them are. It's nearly impassable. A few more hours and they will be completely destroyed. You are a lucky young lady. I've found you before my son did."

Colin made a sound in the back of his throat indicating otherwise, but held his silence.

"That's not entirely true. He just tried to smother me with a pillow." Brenna stepped out of Ratava's embrace and ran her palm over her scar.

"Then we must proceed immediately."

Colin leaned against the windowsill and his anger at the situation festered, boiling just below the surface.

"What's going on?" Brenna wrung her hands, and her blood pressure ticked upwards.

"A blood pact," Colin said and exchanged a knowing glance with Ratava.

Merlin pranced into the study, clearly excited he'd found his mistress. He strutted up to Ratava like a peacock and checked out the prevailing scents emanating from the king's ankles. He shifted his weight slightly to free a hind leg for lifting.

"Merlin, don't you dare."

Weighing his options, the little beast relented and sauntered to sit at Colin's feet, leaving Ratava unmarked. For now.

"What do you mean, a blood pact?" Brenna said.

"Yes, one that will grant you the gift of magic. Normally, you'd have to practice long hours to perfect your new abilities. But in this case, I'm imparting to you my skills with magic, so that you will be able to protect yourself from Hafnar. As a king, I am able to make this pact."

Brenna shook her head. Disbelieving. "If you're here, I should be safe with your magic without need of my own."

"We need an offensive strategy, and this will provide such a solution," Colin said.

"Well, it would be a relief to be able to protect myself from Hafnar." Her logical mind agreed with Colin's conclusion, but she didn't like being rushed into a decision. She pinched the line of the ragged scar on her cheek and felt the heat rise from her chest to her neck to her face. Even her earlobes pulsed with her elevated blood pressure. "How long do I have to think about it?"

"Miss Sinclair, ye can pretend ye have a choice to make, but ye don't, so let's get this done." Colin moved to his desk, opened a drawer and removed an ornately carved wooden box. He flicked open the latch and swung open the cover. Nestled in black velvet lay a dagger. Etched on the blade was a dragon's tail and on the handle the carved body of the beast, a heart clutched in its talons.

He handed the weapon to Ratava.

"It will be painless, I'll see to that, so don't fret over the cut," Ratava said.

True to his word, Brenna didn't feel a thing when the king sliced one palm then the other. Then he turned the blade on himself. He tossed the blade to Colin, who wiped it clean with a cloth and returned it to its velvet bed.

"Join hands," Ratava said.

The moment her hand clasped that of the king, tingles of warmth ran up Brenna's arms, across her chest, and down to her toes. Her heart felt like it would burst from the confines of her chest.

Blood oozed from their joined hands and drops formed like morning dew. They fell with a splat onto the hardwood floor. Merlin bounded over to investigate. He lapped up the drops before anyone could stop him.

Ratava released her hands, and she watched in amazement as the traces of blood slithered into the dagger's cut and disappeared, and the wounds knitted seamlessly closed.

Ratava looked at her encouragingly. "Try using your magic, Brenna."

"All right. I'm going to make this God awful pounding headache go away, and if that works, I'm going to mend my arm. How does it work?"

"The magic is quite simple. Form the thought in your mind and execute the thought," Ratava said.

Brenna closed her eyes and pictured her headache as a balloon inflated to fill the inside of her head, then she imagined it deflating and vanishing.

And it worked.

"This is incredible, my head doesn't ache anymore." She shook her head from side to side, waiting for the stab of pain and wave of dizziness. Not even a twinge.

"As accident prone as ye are, it's a skill ye'll be using repeatedly." Colin smirked at her and Jen snickered in the background.

"Is the magic permanent? Will I always have it now?"

"A human's blood supply is gradually replaced by the body over a 120 day period. The magic will be strongest now and fade as red blood cells are replaced. We'll reevaluate when the time comes and consider the necessity of another blood pact."

Brenna turned her attention to her broken arm. This time she isolated the exact location of the break by focusing her mind and pinpointing the spot with the most pain. She imagined each cell on either side of the break reaching out and grasping hold of another. A line of dewy moisture formed on her upper lip, and she licked the salty drops away. Her breathing went shallow as she tunneled her energy on knitting her fractured arm.

She lifted her casted arm in Colin's direction. "Cut this thing off me will you?"

A lopsided grin broke across his face. "Take it off yerself."

A quick flick of her hand, and the cast fell away with a *thud* to the floor.

Brenna picked it up and flung it toward the ceiling and Jen laughed when it burst into a rainbow of confetti. Colin raised an eyebrow at the mess it made of his study.

"Ye'd better be planning to clean that up."

Brenna conjured a whirlwind that sucked up the bits into its vortex and spewed them out the window. She hurried to the embrasure and watched the bits flitter to the ground below.

"Easy peasy," she said and rubbed her hands together, a mile wide grin stretched across her face.

A gust of wind from the open window scattered the papers piled neatly on Colin's desk. A shadow oozed into the room. A dark haze that sharpened and formed into the bastard that was Hafnar.

"Son of a bitch—I need to find a new sorceress," Colin said.

Jen lunged and scooped up a barking Merlin before he got himself kicked or killed. Colin reached behind him, yanked a sword from its slumber on the wall and held it aloft. Jen scuttled behind him for cover. The bastard grinned at them, already counting this encounter as a victory. Not waiting for an invitation, Colin sliced through the air at Hafnar. The faerie deflected the blow with a flick of his hand as if it were no more than a midge. His grin widened and laughter shook him.

“That’s enough, boy,” Ratava said.

Hafnar’s grin settled into a grim line. He turned his back to Colin and faced his father.

Ratava eyed Hafnar coolly. “Didn’t expect to see me here, did you, son?”

Hafnar’s face reddened, and his eyes turned dark and cold. Colin crept closer, brandished the sword again, and caught Hafnar below his shoulder blades, drawing a vivid line of red. Hafnar bellowed and turned, then threw a stream of fire at his attacker. Stepping deftly aside, Colin rolled, Jen crouched with Merlin, and the flame splashed against the stone of the window embrasure. Colin lunged a third time. Hafnar latched onto the sword with his magic and yanked it from Colin’s grip. He launched it over his shoulder without looking.

Ratava reacted to the danger too late. The sword flew in a perfect arc and speared him. Blood spewed from the wound in his chest, and he fell to his knees.

“That sword is iron,” Colin yelled. “Ye’ve bloody killed yer own father.”

A look of shock painted Hafnar’s face, “Father, I didn’t mean—this is your fault, bitch!” He turned to glare at her.

Brenna thought she saw regret in Hafnar’s eyes and time hung suspended between them. He launched at her, catching her arms in a vice grip. Twisting and turning and stomping wildly, Brenna caused his hold to falter. He released her and she threw him an uppercut to the jaw. He used her momentum from the punch to swing her around. He wrapped his meaty arms around her chest and waist and pinned her to him, then shifted them from the room.

###

Brenna didn't move, kept her eyes firmly shut, and concentrated on keeping her breath slow and even. No light leaked past her closed lids. The surface beneath her was hard and cold, leaching the heat from her body. A shiver threatened to convulse through her, and she fought to keep it in check. The stagnant air smelled of dust and neglect.

"Awake are you, love?"

The sound of his voice made her skin crawl. She'd begged Lachlan to turn him over to the Fae council, and he'd begrudgingly agreed. She was through being kind to her enemy. Done. She hated him, enough to kill him. He'd killed his own father. She'd been wrong. He could never be rehabilitated. Lachlan would have his revenge.

She sat up and swung her legs beneath her. The room was barren and devoid of furniture, except for the wooden chair where Hafnar sat. A wave of his hand and heavy drapes parted revealing a too bright sun that blazed in through the open windows. Her eyes watered and she squinted against the brightness. The blood congealed in her veins at the realization they weren't in the Highlands any more.

"Where have you taken me?"

"Welcome to my home, love, where you will be my guest. Indefinitely."

"Where are we?" Brenna asked.

"We are in the world of the Fae. My realm. My kingdom," Hafnar said, sweeping his arms wide.

Fear clawed at her gut with razor sharp talons, and shallow breaths sent her into a fit of hyperventilation. Her knees melted under her weight, and she sank to the stone floor.

"My dear girl, breathe through your nose. Take a deep breath, that's right. Relax. Now, take a look out that window." He gestured toward the window with his hand.

It was stunning.

The sun spewed golden rays over a sapphire ocean, and the sandy shore glittered with pink sand. She'd never seen such a shore before, though she'd been told sand like this existed on Harbour Island in the Bahamas.

A rolling meadow cascaded with yellow blossoms. Acres upon acres of the tiny flowers flowed like an ocean of their own. Dazzling colors burst forth from all directions and enveloped her in sensual delight unimagined in her world.

Whatever manner of building she was in floated a hundred feet above the ground. She glimpsed enormous candy striped ropes tethering the structure, though she could feel it swaying gently in the light breeze.

He'd brought her to Faerie. A butterfly fluttered in her belly. Lachlan was here. Somewhere. Hope flared in her heart. Hafnar had the advantage of his home turf. She had the advantage of surprise. He was oblivious to the Fae magic in her veins. A sigh of relief passed from her lips, and she winked at him.

His gaze faltered for an instant. Her unusual reaction seemed to puzzle him and his eyes turned inky black, one brow rose quizzically.

"Why don't you stay right there, while I get the door?" She thrust her palm at him, shoving an unseen force toward him that flattened him against the back of his chair and kept him immobile in his seat. She threw her other palm outward toward the door and blew it completely off its hinges, splintering the solid oak into needle sharp slivers. Shocked, he struggled against her power.

A crooked finger wagged at the pile of rubble and coaxed a handful of wood fragments into her cupped hand. She threw them violently along with a stream of magic and hoped they were sharp enough to imbed in his flesh.

A howl like a rabid wolf tore through the chamber. Uncontrolled laughter rocked Brenna, her stress response in high gear. "Oh God, that was a good one, wasn't it? You look like a porcupine." She pointed at him and clutched her stomach to keep from doubling over.

"How is it you have magic?"

"Your father gave it to me, so I could kick your sorry ass the next time you pulled a stunt. And here we are. Ready?"

Anger dissolved her fear, and anguish gave her strength. The magic still bound him and she toppled the chair backwards with a powerful wave of her hand. Hafnar's head struck the stone floor a reverberating blow.

Hafnar shook himself. Brenna had time to collect herself before he fought back with a blast of power directed her way. Her newfound magic waivered. Hafnar quickly recovered and cast a bolt of lightning toward her and then scrambled to his feet. Static electricity engulfed her, and the air smelled of ozone. She threw a river of water at him to draw the direction of his next bolt. It worked. She remained unscathed by the lightning, but it struck the center of the room and blasted a three-foot hole in the floor. Fragments of stone flew in all directions, fraying the tether ropes and the castle swayed violently.

Shouts sounded from the living quarters above. Were they enemies on their way to destroy her? The magic was taking its toll. Jittery legs threatened to topple her, and a fog settled over her. She couldn't think straight. Fear niggled at her concentration, and she struggled to decide what to do next. *Fight.*

The gaping hole of the doorway and stairwell beckoned. *No time.* She waved her hand and enormous snakes, fifteen feet long and as thick as telephone poles, slithered out of her imagination and into the stairwell. Behind them, she conjured boulders from the air and piled them as far up the passageway as she could to make descending the stairwell impossible. Then she summoned a steel door six inches thick and sealed the passage. The effort dropped her, panting and out of breath, to her knees. Ratava hadn't mentioned that exhaustion would overcome her.

A ring of fire sprouted from the floor and surrounded her. The stones beneath her feet sizzled from the white-hot flames. Brenna's skin blistered, and she would swear her blood bubbled in her veins. The walls of the dungeon shivered and strained. The weight of the boulders she'd used to block the stairwell exceeded the limits of the room's construction. She blew a stream of ice from her lungs, freezing the flames, turning them into a structure any ice carver would be proud of. The room tilted precariously as its Faerie engineering failed. In a last ditch effort, Brenna conjured two handfuls of needle sharp iron filings and hurled them at Hafnar.

Bullseye.

His howl followed her as she dove through the gaping hole in the floor and prayed the fall wouldn't kill her. She thought of tiny Tessa's gossamer light wings and how little effort it took for the Faerie dragon to fly. Exhausted beyond measure, she imagined wings sprouting from her shoulders. A glance behind her confirmed it.

No wings.

Failure, a hundred feet below, waited to collect her body when it broke upon impact. Her thoughts fractured. Jen holding her hand through every miserable moment in her adult life; Colin insisting she could not fail, holding her like a wayward child when she cried; and Lachlan, loving her beyond measure.

Lachlan. She'd freed him and had felt his passion free her. It was worth every risk, worth dying for.

I love you all, more than anything.

A *screech* shattered the sky. A lonely, painful cry of despair. It knocked her from her free fall course to death and strong arms wrapped her tightly. Golden beams of sunlight glittered off the turquoise scales covering the beast.

Soren.

She closed her eyes and breathed.

###

Lachlan ran a hand through his hair and scrubbed his face once Brenna was safely in Soren's grasp. Ariel stood steadfast at his side along with the captain of the guard, and they watched from the ground as the castle swayed and the dungeon disintegrated stone by stone. The ruckus had drawn them from the king's study only to find serpents slithering from the stairwell, and boulders blocking their path.

Soren hovered above him and released Brenna into his waiting arms, rounding back for Hafnar, should he fall from the sky like a dying star. Lachlan placed Brenna on the meadow grass. She babbled incoherently and writhed in pain. Ariel brushed the hair out of her face and revealed the burns on her face, then set to work healing the wounds.

"Lachlan, look at this." She pulled her hands away as if Brenna's skin seared her fingertips. They watched in fascination as the tender pink flesh undulated across her face like a living thing. Rising and falling like swells of the ocean.

Lachlan turned her head slightly. "The scar on her cheek. It's gone." Lachlan traced the path from the corner of her eye to the corner of her mouth where the furious arc had been. One by one the blistered burns disappeared and revealed cream-colored skin beneath.

"She has magic." Ariel stared at him with disbelieving eyes. "Fae blood runs in her veins."

Above them, Soren's shrill cry rang out. A burning body streaked through the sky. One swipe of the dragon's talon's yanked Hafnar from the free fall. He glided silently through the air and dropped Hafnar the last few feet to land next to the others. Soren landed atop him and pinned Hafnar's arms beneath his muscled forelegs. Regan pulled out an arrow and knocked it in his crossbow.

Ariel turned to Hafnar to assess the damage. Burned beyond recognition, tiny metal slivers protruded from every inch of exposed skin. She tugged one, cried out, and flung the shard away.

"Iron. These will kill him." Ariel's voice held a hint of compassion. Ariel looked to Soren, then Lachlan.

Soren shifted to his human form and waited for Lachlan's command. Lachlan nodded his head. Soren moved beside Ariel. Unaffected by iron, he began plucking the shards from Hafnar's body.

Lachlan enfolded Brenna in the cocoon of his arms. She shifted in his embrace and regained consciousness.

Her fists flailed against his chest, pounding out her frustration. "Let me go. I can't kill him if you don't let me go."

"Ye wanted him turned over to the Fae Council, lass, don't ye remember?"

"They can't possibly punish him enough for what he's done. He killed your father. Damn you, Lachlan, let me go!"

A thunderous cracking sliced the air, and the dungeon succumbed to the burden of the boulders, raining down on the meadow below. Dust and bits of debris whorled in erratic patterns then settled quietly into the slumber of the dead. Brenna stopped struggling against Lachlan's hold, curled into his chest, and he rocked her like a child.

"I doubt that, lass. My father is a difficult man to kill. His enemies have tried for years and failed."

"He was run through with an iron sword. I was there, I saw it."

"Are ye sure, lass?"

"Yes. Lachlan, I'm so sorry, but he's gone."

"Hafnar's waking," Regan said.

Lachlan left her side, manacles jangling from where they hung at his belt. He looked down at the man who'd wreaked havoc on his life. Bile rose in his throat and burned his lungs. He secured Hafnar's wrists and ankles with the manacles. The runes inscribed in the cuffs would render his Fae powers useless, just as he had been helpless all those centuries in the cavern. All the days and nights he'd thought about the revenge he would exact upon this man, and the day had at last arrived.

Brenna had given her assent. He didn't require her permission, but certainly hadn't expected it. How does a man beat a half dead dog and find any pleasure in the blows?

He couldn't do it.

He stared at the torque that had been his before his banishment to the cavern. It left behind an angry red mark when he yanked it from Hafnar's neck. He slipped it around his own and felt a jolt of strength. It flooded through his veins, vigor infused his entire body, and the sudden power knocked him to his knees.

Soren stood, his chest heaving with the effort to refrain from annihilating the half dead Fae at his feet. Smoke whorled from his nostrils and liquid silver eyes pinned Lachlan, awaiting his orders.

Standing to issue his command, Lachlan said, "We leave immediately for the council. Knock him out." A flick of his hand would suffice, but he owed the dragon at least one pleasure.

Brenna reached out her hand, and Lachlan helped her to her feet.

A hundred yards away, the ground shook and violent cracks of lightening extended from the earth to the sky. Intermittent flames spewed into the sky like volcano eruptions.

Her legs shook beneath her, and he clutched her to his body. "I love ye more than my life, lass; but ye must go. Those flames mark the portal. It's nearly destroyed, we're searching for a way to repair it. Our magic can't sustain it. You must go. It may not be able to transport you home even now. And if Father is truly dead as ye say, then my kingdom awaits me."

"But I don't want to go. I'll stay here with you, we can be together here."

"Nay, lass. Ye cannot stay. Our laws forbid it. Ye'll be a marked woman. It'll only be a matter of time before the Dark Fae hunt ye down like a rabid dog." He tucked an errant lock of auburn hair behind her ear and ran his thumb along her cheekbone, then planted his palm behind her neck and pulled her to him. She traced her hands across his chest, and his heartbeat thudded under her touch. He had known the insanity of captivity, the lust for revenge, but the love he felt for this woman he would take through eternity. His mouth captured hers and passion stirred his loins. The smell of lavender wafted from her hair, and her lips tasted of honey. Each detail he committed to memory. The heat sizzled between them, not a breath of air separated their bodies.

Lachlan ended the kiss while he still had his wits. "Regan, take her. Get her through the portal. Go—hurry."

Regan grabbed Brenna's arm and ran headlong for the passage. They didn't slow down, not for an instant.

"Lachlan—" Her agonized scream exploded through the meadow.

Regan headed directly toward the flames that ringed a small section of grass. Brenna hesitated, but he pulled her along mercilessly. The strength of his vice grip made her cry out, but he didn't slow. If anything, he ran faster.

Another tremor shook the ground. Regan crossed the flaming circle and enfolded Brenna in a steel embrace. They were in the portal. The ground fell out from beneath their feet and sent them into a free fall Brenna was sure would kill them. The whoosh of rushing air blocked out the sound of her scream and swallowed it like a black hole. Lightning flashed, brushing past them, and the stink of ozone filled the portal. Pressure built within the walls of the passage and squeezed closer on the verge of imploding. Regan held her tighter, his grip never faltered. A sonic boom heralded their arrival into the mortal realm and the ground greeted them with a *thud.*

They were safe. And alive.

###

The exhaustion from using her magic and the narrow escape from Faerie seeped bone deep, but the loss of Lachlan took hold of her heart and cleaved it. When she woke, a cadre of faces surrounded her bed, all eyes upon her.

Clearly, her descent into the depths of despair was being cut short. A cold nose poked her cheek, and Merlin wagged his body in greeting, then tucked up next to her and sighed.

Jen sat on the edge of the bed and took her hand. "Are you okay, Bren?"

"King Ratava…he didn't survive, did he?" Brenna asked. She questioned what her own eyes had seen.

Jen raked her fingers through her hair, a sure sign she was nervous. "No. His wounds were fatal. The king is dead."

Colin shoved away from the wall where he'd been propped, crossed the room to Brenna and gave her arm a gentle squeeze. "It was his fate, planned out for him long before any of us existed."

He'd had so little time with his son. She wished she'd had more time to know him. "What happens now?" Brenna asked.

"Protocol requires he be buried in the Hall of Kings in Faerie. But the portal is completely destroyed. There's no way to get him back to his realm. We've decided to bury him at Lachlan's castle ruins."

Lachlan.

Time stopped and reality settled over her like a death shroud. She would never see Lachlan again.

No.

Brenna closed her eyes and reached for him with her mind.

Nothing.

Again.

Nothing.

Tears leaked from her eyes. For years she'd hoped that her gift would magically disappear in much the same manner as it originally appeared. Now that she'd found the one person in the world she *wanted* to connect with, the universe chose this time to honor her wish.

###

The days passed one after the other in the orderly succession that was time. Brenna mourned her loss while Jen and Colin did their best to buoy her spirits, and Regan kept a constant vigil at her door. Not once did he complain about being cut off from his home. Time and time again she reached for Lachlan only to be met with empty silence.

For weeks, Brenna clutched at the small hope that remained in her heart. That Lachlan would find a way to repair the portal and they could be together. That he'd find another passage, that this was all a horrible, horrible dream.

Finally, she let the fantasy drift away on the late summer breeze. Fall crept closer and the crisp air stirred her thoughts toward a new season in her life. She couldn't bear to leave and return home to the States. Her heart was here, in the Highlands. She spent time each day alone, at the castle ruins, remembering happier days spent with Lachlan. She even learned to pray amidst the crumbling chapel. At last, she made up her mind in the late days of August.

"I've decided to resign my post at the university," she announced at dinner.

Jen dropped her fork and it clunked to the floor. Merlin whisked it away to his bed near the great hall hearth to lick it clean.

"Aye. So will ye be staying here awhile longer then?" Colin asked.

"Yes. That is, if you don't mind. I'm happy to find a place in town if it's inconvenient," she said in her most business like voice. "I'd like to be close to the castle, though. I've decided to ask for a grant from a historical society to restore it." Her voice drifted to a whisper, and she pushed her food around in her plate.

"Ye'll stay here. And for what it's worth, I think it would please Lachlan that ye want to restore his castle. I know just the architect to help ye with the project. He can even help ye with the grant writing. He's familiar with the process and has been quite successful in helping his clients secure the proper funding."

"I'm sorry, Jen. I hope you understand. I need to stay."

Jen's lips quivered, but she managed a smile. "You'd better invite me back for Christmas."

"Deal," Brenna said.

Colin raised his glass. "Well, then, let us toast to new beginnings."

###

Two days later, Colin wondrously produced a ticket to a sold out flight, the one that would see Jen home. She and Brenna had stayed awake most of the night, talking of plans for the future, laying the groundwork that would maintain their sisterhood.

Brenna watched the sleek black limo crunch up the drive. Colin whisked away the luggage, leaving the door open for Jen to follow. Everything that needed to be said, they'd said the night before.

"I'll see you soon," Brenna said and smiled.

Jen nodded in agreement and they hugged. Brenna escorted her friend to the door and stood stoic in the doorway as the limo drove away.

She had one more secret that she hadn't shared with anyone.

CHAPTER TWENTY

September.

CHAPTER TWENTY ONE

October.

CHAPTER TWENTY TWO

November.

Brenna visited the castle ruins each day, though work on its restoration had ended for the winter. The chapel neared completion, waiting only the stained glass windows that would adorn the north-facing wall, blushing the swells of the sea in a swath of color as one gazed at the turbulent water from inside the stone edifice. For now, sheets of plastic kept out the weather.

Thanksgiving was just a week away, and though purely an American holiday, Brenna insisted they celebrate with a traditional feast. Colin had allowed his staff to return from their holiday and Cook relished the idea of a celebration. Brenna and Cook had spent hours together planning the menu, drinking tea, and gossiping. Cook had even coaxed laughter from Brenna, something she thought impossible after her loss.

The weatherman reported conditions were perfect for the rare phenomena known as thunder snow, and Brenna could hear the first rumblings as the front blew closer. Pleasantly plump flakes fell from the ironclad sky.

She stroked Sidra's neck, calming her as they rode toward the chapel. A crack of lightening splintered down from the sky and slapped the ground. For a moment, she contemplated turning around and heading back to the warmth of the manor house, but she relished her time here and decided a few minutes wouldn't harm her.

Despite its size, the chapel door swung open easily. Once inside, she barred it against the wind and snow and took a seat near the altar. She rubbed the gentle swell of her belly reassuringly. The first trimester had passed, and along with it, most of the morning sickness. She removed a small leather journal from the fur-lined cloak Colin had given her. Fearful her memories of Lachlan would fade as the years passed, she chronicled each day they'd spent together so their unborn child would know its father.

She would have to move on soon. Away from the memories that haunted her. They were too new, too raw with emotion. Once she tucked the memories safely away in the journal, she would put them aside for a while. Until she could look back and remember their time with fondness. Not with the knife-edged pain of loss stabbing her. But for now, she ignored the pain and scribbled in her notebook. The pen couldn't scratch fast enough for her thoughts.

The pounding of thundering hooves carried through the glassless windows. A glance at her watch and Brenna realized she'd been nearly two hours in the chapel, lost in her memories. Colin had no doubt given up waiting for her return and come to get her. He'd watched her like an overprotective grizzly since she announced her pregnancy.

An inch of snow greeted her outside, and she waited by Sidra for Colin to appear. He would help her mount. The sound of hoof beats grew louder and an obsidian destrier cleared the stone passageway and entered the castle keep. Enbarr kicked up a swirl of snow in his wake.

Lachlan.

The cloak he wore billowed behind him as he closed the space between them. Longer than she remembered, his unbound raven hair whipped across his face. Her breath clinched her lungs, and her stomach somersaulted. She pinched herself to make sure it wasn't a dream.

He reined in next to Sidra and jumped from Enbarr's back before the monster horse halted. Jeweled eyes froze the words in her throat, and a moment later, his tongue parted her lips, and an ember burst into flame low in her belly. He held her face between his palms, and she grasped his forearms, afraid he'd slip through her fingers.

Lachlan pulled away and rested his forehead against hers. "I've missed ye, lass.

Brenna choked on a sob. "Lachlan." She kissed him then, unsure and not caring if he was real.

At the next pause, he whispered against her mouth, "Never again will I leave yer side, nor will ye leave mine. Yer my heart, my soul, my love."

"How did you get here?" she asked.

"Ariel gathered the most powerful Fae in the land. From all four royal houses, and they conjured enough power to send me here. One trip through is all they could manage. I had to risk the journey. I had to be with ye, Brenna."

Laughing, crying, she gasped for air, but wouldn't turn her lips from his. "How long can you stay?"

"Forever, if ye'll have me."

"I can't believe it. You're here. You're really here. I thought I'd never see you again." Brenna rested her cheek against his chest.

"Father recorded his last wishes." He pulled her away and kissed her forehead. "That Ariel ascend to the throne." He kissed her eyelids. "That I may choose my future." He kissed her cheek. "The Fae council granted me mortality, so I could spend the rest of my life—" He kissed her nose. "—with you." He took her lips again.

The heat of his kiss set fire to her loins. The child within her seemed to sense her joy and kicked.

"What of Hafnar?"

"The council sentenced him to one thousand years, chained to the bottom of the ocean." He nuzzled her neck and trailed a path of kisses to her ear.

"A sentence worse than death. The council showed no mercy," Brenna said

"He deserved none. What say ye, lass? Will ye have me?"

"Yes." She placed his hand on her swollen belly. "And I'd say you'd best marry me before our child is born."

###

Christmas day arrived with a blustering wind blowing in off the North Sea and a foot of fresh snow cloaking the ground. Boughs of evergreen draped the chapel pews and torches lent their light to the stone walls of the vestry.

Regan had done a fine job of conjuring Brenna's gown the night before. Ivory velvet draped her with warmth and gold thread glistened in the dim glow of the torches. The fabric flowed gently over the swell of her pregnancy, though it didn't conceal her condition, she didn't care. She'd gladly announce it from the highest craig in the Highlands.

The portal to Faerie, remained impassible, but the Seer stones allowed Ariel and Soren to share in the joy of this day. They were all here. The strangers who'd welcomed her, believed in her, and risked their very lives to help her save the man who stood waiting for her at the steps of the altar.

"Are ye ready, Miss Sinclair?" Colin slipped her hand to the crook of his arm.

"I've never been more ready for anything in my life." She beamed at him.

Winter Sprites danced across the strings of a harp and Colin escorted her down the aisle. Jen stood at the altar looking demure in a sapphire gown.

Next to Merlin at the front of the church sat a fawn colored Chihuahua they named Nimue. No one could say where she came from, but Brenna suspected Merlin conjured her with the few drops of blood he'd lapped up on the day she'd gained her magic. Regan gifted the tiny girl with a bauble that dangled from her neck.

Colin kissed her cheek and handed her to Lachlan, then stood beside him as best man. At last, her gaze rested on her Faerie prince. His eyes danced with fire and saw through to her very soul. Warmth spread outward from her heart and lifted her lips in a smile.

Lachlan tucked a curl behind her ear and broke protocol with a kiss for the bride before the vows. "I couldn't help myself. Ye're more lovely than I've ever seen ye."

The ceremony passed in a blur, and Lachlan kissed her again. He swept her up and turned circles with her in his arms. "Yer mine now, Brenna. I'll cherish ye all the days of my life."

ACKNOWLEDGEMENTS

As with most books, *Of Magic and The Sea* was not an individual effort. Although writing is often a solitary endeavor, it takes a small tribe to beat errant words on the page into some semblance of order. This novel would never have seen the light of day, (that cliche is for you Gabs) without the encouragement, the support, and the tough love of my critique partner Gabi Anderson. A fabulous author and a true friend, I would never have made this book a reality without you. I thank you for everything. Truly.

I extend my greatest sympathy to the first two readers of my work, Tamra Baumann who suffered through passive voice out the wazoo, and Karen Mauldin who read those early drafts (of which there have been six, by the way). You both encouraged me to continue on this silly venture to publish a book. I'd have given up long ago without the two of you.

Great big hugs to Brenda, Sheley, and Barb, my Kickass Wild Women Sisterhood who support me in all things. You gals rock it!

DON'T FORGET

If you enjoyed this novel, take a sec and leave a review so other readers may benefit from your insight.

http://bit.ly/AddisonKayne

ABOUT THE AUTHOR

Addison Kayne is an award-winning author who writes contemporary paranormal romance with kilt-wearing Scottish heroes. Always a voracious reader, Addison snatched her first romance novel from her mother's stash and has been hooked on happily-ever-after stories ever since. She lives in the desert Southwest, where the sun shines 360 days a year and a rainy day is cause for celebration. She fell in love with her soulmate from a photograph and moved two thousand miles from her hometown to be with him. Twenty-something years later, they're still having fun! They are now the proud parents of three adorable fur babies, two of whom you'll meet in Addison's novel, *Of Magic and The Sea.*

Stop by and say "Hi" at: www.AddisonKayne.com

To be notified of her next release or sign up for her newsletter here:
http://www.addisonkayne.com/newsletter

Made in the USA
San Bernardino, CA
26 November 2018